Dear Ken
I hope
you
enjoy it

TARIQ

I KNOW
TWO SUDANS

*An Anthology of creative writing
from Sudan and South Sudan*

EDITED BY:
DJAMELA MAGID | AMAL OSMAN
ROD USHER | ALI ABDULLA ALI RAMRAM

3

This paperback edition published 2014 by Gipping Press Ltd
Gipping Press Ltd, Units 1&2 Lion Barn Ind. Estate,
Needham Market, Ipswich, Suffolk IP6 8NZ

ISBN 978-0-9931108-0-1

First published in the United Kingdom in 2014.

Second Impression November 2014

Third Impression July 2015

Fourth Impression January 2016

This book is the result of an innovative writing project, Creative Writing from the Sudans. The project attempted to attract creative writing from a wide range of Sudanese and others who had memorable experiences in the Sudans and have developed a love of the land and its peoples.

Much of the current writing about the Sudans is negative and yet those who know the Sudans will realise that these stories are only part of the true picture of a vast land rich in heritage and a variety of cultures, languages and ethnic groups.

There is so much to know about the Sudans and their peoples.

Most of the stories in this book were shortlisted from competition entries. The winners selected by Leila Aboulela were as follows:

Stella Gaitano, *A Lake the Size of a Papaya Fruit* (First Prize)
David L. Lukudo, *Ahmed Suk Suk* (Second Prize)
Mohamed Fakhreldin Omer, *Greeting Khaltu Fatma* (Third Prize)

Elizabeth Harrison, *The Patient Ones* (Honourable Mention)
Reem Gaafar, *The Light in the Dessert* (Honourable Mention)

Acknowledgements

The Editors would like to thank Leila Aboulela for participating in this project and dedicating her care and attention to choosing the winners. We would also like to thank Nadir El Gadi for his generous support, and to everybody else who contributed to our funds and made publication possible.

Many thanks to Jenni Pinnock and Jagdish Lall for creating our website and poster respectively. Thank you to The Youth Factor, 500 Words Magazine, Nas with Notepads and Anna Rowett in South Sudan for promoting our project and spreading the word.

Thank you to Julia Usher for commissioning the maps from www.themappingcompany.co.uk and to Sara Asim for sponsoring all the artwork. We are grateful to the artists, Hussein Merghani and Mutaz Mohamed, for allowing us to use their work.

Finally, we are grateful to Jonathan at Gipping Press, whose guidance in the printing of this book we could not have done without.

Chosen Charities

All the proceeds from the sale of this book will be equally divided between two children's charities.

The Children of Sudan is a UK registered charity that was brought together by a group of young people living in the United Kingdom. The aim of the organisation is to better the future of the youth of Sudan. The Children of Sudan helps provide decent education, efficient healthcare, child sponsorship programmes and integrate youth projects for children all over Sudan, regardless of their race, religion or socio-economic background.

Confident Children out of Conflict is a South Sudanese NGO based in Juba. It has established a safe center where survivors of gender based violence and girls at risk of sexual exploitation and abuse, who come from the slums, internally displaced people's camps, and streets, are protected and reintegrated back into society by providing life skills, physical, social and psychosocial guidance. Its vision is to create a safe and just environment, which enables orphans, vulnerable children and young adults, to emerge from conflict and give them the opportunity to develop confidence in their own capabilities to have a meaningful future and contribute to a peaceful South Sudan.

Already £1,000 has been given to each of the above two charities named.

Sales of the book have surpassed expectations. Consequently, in addition to these two substantial donations a further donation has been made to a mother and baby refuge in Khartoum, founded and managed by Nur, who features in the remarkable book "Daughter of Dust".

Income from future sales of "I know two Sudans" will be donated to children's charities in both Khartoum and Juba.

Contents

INTRODUCTION

It was while on holiday in Sudan, the year before last, that the seeds of the idea for this book were first sown in my mind. I was there for my cousin's wedding, a three-day extravaganza. Between that, trips to the Nile, maghrib tea with my grandmother and breakfast on Fridays with my extended family, including thirteen of my first cousins, there was never a dull moment.

Meanwhile I was reading Chimamanda Ngozi Adichie's *The Thing Around Your Neck* and drawing parallels between her Nigerian culture and mine in Sudan. What struck me the most was that despite the elements of sadness, tragedy and diasporic struggles that permeate her narratives, the book gives you a real sense of her love for her country. I considered how wonderful it would be to create something similar about Sudan and, simultaneously, what a shame it is that my writing skills are nothing like Adichie's.

It was in this way that the idea to collect the pieces and to hold a competition came about and that has been for the best. I could never have represented Sudan and South Sudan, or done justice to such a wonderfully varied land, in the same way that all the writers of the stories in this book have done. Likewise, I could never have set-up or achieved the Creative Writing from the Sudans project, which led to this book, without unwavering commitment and enthusiasm from Amal, Rod and Ali, who, alongside myself, make up the team and editors of this work.

The four of us have in common admiration for the two Sudans and their diverse peoples. We have endeavoured to compile a work that reflects this and as such we have chosen to look beyond political and religious concerns. It is not that we don't care, or that we think they should be ignored. On the contrary, we all hold strong personal points of view and we have all been particularly concerned about events in South Sudan over recent months. We sought to reflect this, albeit in the smallest way, by extending the deadline for the competition. The lack of political and religious content means the book is missing a large and significant part of life in the Sudans, but it has also enabled us to include pieces about other, equally significant, aspects of the two countries.

This book, made possible by family, friends and strangers, is my love letter to a land I have held, and will always hold, dear. I hope you will enjoy reading it as much as my teammates and I have enjoyed putting it together.

Djamela
June 2014

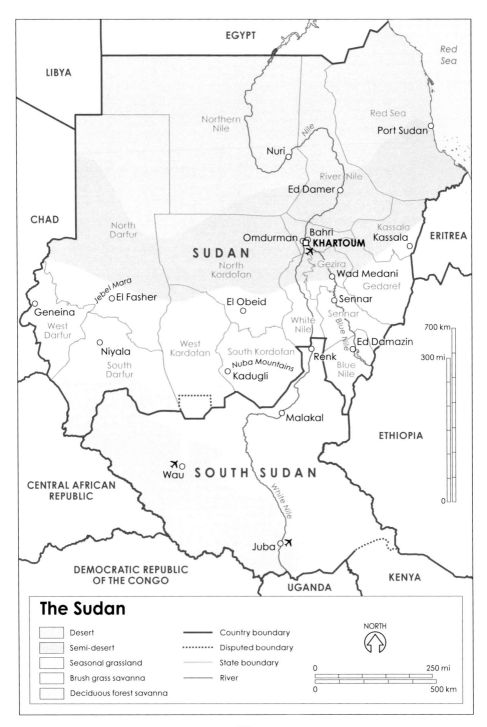

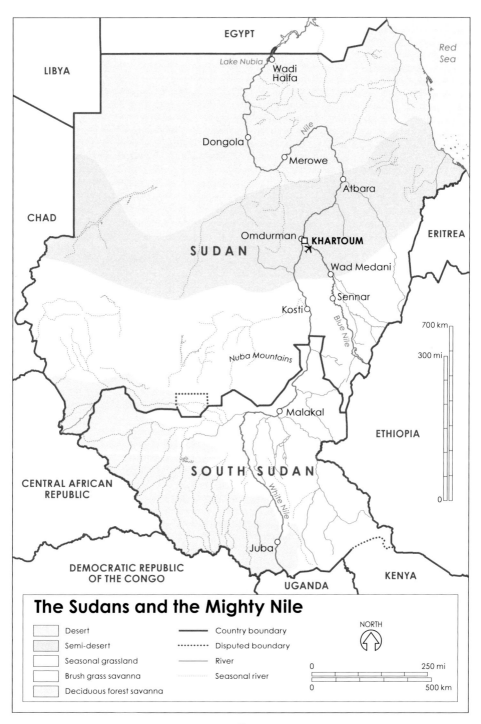

The Sudans and the Mighty Nile

Desert
Semi-desert
Seasonal grassland
Brush grass savanna
Deciduous forest savanna

Country boundary
Disputed boundary
River
Seasonal river

NORTH

EGYPT
LIBYA
Lake Nubia
Wadi Halfa
Dongola
Merowe
Nile
Atbara
CHAD
Omdurman □ KHARTOUM
S U D A N
Wad Medani
Sennar
Kosti
Blue Nile
ERITREA
Red Sea
700 km
300 mi
Nuba Mountains
Malakal
ETHIOPIA
CENTRAL AFRICAN
REPUBLIC
S O U T H   S U D A N
White Nile
Juba
DEMOCRATIC REPUBLIC
OF THE CONGO
UGANDA
KENYA

0 _____ 250 mi
0 _____ 500 km

Omdurman □ **KHARTOUM** ✈

Nile

Blue Nile

S U D A N

Abyei

Upper
Nile

Malakal ✈

North
Bahr-al-
Ghazal

Unity

West
Bahr-al-
Ghazal

Kuajok ○
○ Ajiep

ETHIOPIA

Warab

Jungoli

Wau ✈

S O U T H   S U D A N

Rumbek ○
Lakes

White Nile

**CENTRAL
AFRICAN
REPUBLIC**

West Equatoria

Eastern
Equatoria

Juba ○ ✈

Central
Equatoria

KENYA

**DEMOCRATIC REPUBLIC
OF THE CONGO**

UGANDA

500 km

200 mi

0

South Sudan

Desert	Country boundary	
Semi-desert	Disputed boundary	
Seasonal grassland	State boundary	
Brush grass savanna	River	
Deciduous forest savanna	Seasonal river	

NORTH

| 0 | | 150 mi |
| 0 | | 300 km |

MANOUTE: THE SPECIAL BLESSING

by Waddah Jaffar Hassan Abbass

He had been part of our lives all the time, I still remember him taking me on his back; accompanying me to the shop or to the sports club near the house. Out of my mother's 17 siblings, Manoute[1] was the only person my age in my grandmother's house, where we spent our summer vacation every year. My grandmother's house, which still exists, is a very big house. It consists of a compound type building that houses my uncles and aunts, none of whom are close to me in needs or interests like Manoute.

As the days passed my friendship with Manoute grew closer than ever. During my holidays he used to show me all around the city, and take me to football games. Manoute was fervent of basketball. Although I was a good footballer, I was touched by his passion for basketball. He, therefore, started teaching me the rules and fundamentals of the game in the rusty neighborhood court. Together we used to play PlayStation basketball games, watch games on live television, and videos. We could hardly separate from each other. His passion for the game was driven by his spiritual superlative model; his uncle, Manoute Bol, the famous Sudanese American basketball player. He was proud to be named after him, and that he looked so much like him, dark and tall. He dreamed of one day being able to travel to America to be a professional basketball player and join the NBA.

I spent a lot of time reading to Manoute junior about his uncle Manoute senior on the internet; his character, his big shots, his charity efforts and continuous support for Southern Sudanese refugee camps.

From both Manoute and my uncle Osman, I learned his story. Manoute originated from an area where there was civil war and tribal unrest in the southern part of Sudan. He was found in a refugee camp in Abyei by my uncle, who worked as a local government inspector for UNICEF at that time. Abyei is a border city in the South of Sudan which used to host the largest refugee camp in the area. My uncle described the camp as an area which was largely affected by famine, and held more than 5,000 child refugees who lived in hunger and suffered from malnutrition and various deficiencies. He also stated that there was hardly any place to sleep in the camp, and that corpses of children surrounded the area with stray dogs feeding off the little meat on the corpses. The bond between Manoute and my uncle during his stay in the refugee camp grew very strong.

When my uncle Osman's mission in Abyei ended he took Manoute, a child of 8 years, to Jebel Aulia to live with my family. From then he was considered part of the family. My mum told me that my grandfather took him to school and followed-up his studies. He showed a great desire to learn and succeeded to be the top of his class because he was older than the rest of the students. Unfortunately, for the same reason Manoute left the school as he had grown very tall while the other students were very short compared to him.

Later I found out that Manoute, after great efforts, found his mother and sisters, and that he had to be evacuated from the North due to the recent separation of the North

---

1. Manoute means special blessing in the language of the Dinka

and South of Sudan, despite all endeavors made by my uncle Osman to resist evacuation. Manoute was unable to stay mainly due to the fact that his mother wanted him to join his family and get married when he was just 17.

During my last summer vacation in Sudan, I greatly missed my mate Manoute. His shadow was following me around the big house and everywhere I went. It was just then I remembered how sad his glance was. His story always reminded me of many fictitious stories I read about lost children in different places of the globe, stories about unhappy childhood, separation from family, friends, culture and one's own people and race. It was never easy not to see such a close friend like him. I would think that maybe it was for his own good, and fulfillment of his dream of being a professional international basketball player would be my only comfort. I will never give up thinking of meeting him and seeing him again.

About the author:

My name is Waddah Abbas. I am a Sudanese law student who grew up in Qatar, and currently studying in Leeds. I had written this piece as part of an application process for university.

BABY LOVE
by Leila Aboulela

We were going to the Hilton. I wasn't sure whether to wear my denim skirt or a dress. Better wear a dress, my pink one with the belt. I liked belts - that's what I liked about my school uniform, its white belt. My dress needed ironing so I had to open the kitchen window and shout for Ali to do it. He must have been asleep because he took ages to answer. 'Hurry', I told him when he appeared. I still couldn't get used to seeing him without that lump on his eyebrow that was as big as a Ping-Pong ball. My father had paid for the operation to remove it and Ali came back from the hospital smiling and very pleased with himself. Lately though, he'd developed higher aspirations and didn't want to be a houseboy anymore. At the end of the month he was going to leave us and become an electrician.

I polished my nails Aubergine and remembered to clean my sandals. It was half past one, thirty-one minutes past one. She wouldn't, like Sameer, park and ring the doorbell. She would blow the car horn and I mustn't rush out and seem too keen. Lunch at the Hilton, I was keen. It would be Open Buffet, eat as much as you like. But today with my future mother-in-law, I had no intention of eating as much as I liked. She would be shocked.

A car horn. I leapt up from the sofa and checked my face again in the hall mirror. I shouted, 'Ali, I'm going' and walked as slowly as I could down the garden path.

'Hi,' I couldn't call her Auntie because she didn't like it. Because she was African-American she wanted me to call her Janet, but it was so rude. So I didn't call her anything and whenever I spoke about her to Sameer I said 'your mom'.

'Hi, Majda. Just look at your pretty dress!' Her voice was rich and deep though she was delicately built, with slender arms. I loved the way she pronounced my name. I loved her American accent.

She drove fast, confident. When I asked about Uncle Kamal, who I could thankfully call Uncle, she said, 'He's having lunch with his sister- gobbledygook.'

I laughed. She hated Sudanese food, except for kebab. She hated cumin and we put cumin in everything. The food she cooked was deliberate and slightly sweet. When she made salad she said, 'I threw together a salad'.

I rolled up the window so the wind wouldn't mess up my hair. I thought of the smooth, air-conditioned lobby of the Hilton, my sandals on the marbled floor, white tablecloths and napkins.

'Sam called last night,' she said.

'Oh, why didn't he call me too?' I sounded childish and envious.

'He said he tried you but you were out.'

'Ali is so stupid', I said, 'I was at the neighbours next door. He could have fetched me.'

'It's just as well he didn't do that, Majda. Long-distance calls are expensive and you guys chat for so long even though Sam's on a student budget,' she clicked on the indicator to turn left into Airport Road. It was a loud clicking noise, louder than any other car I've been in.

I went on, 'Ali just shouts. 'Out, out, they're all out' and slams down the phone. We never know who called us…'

'Well, why don't you give Sam a call tonight?'

It's funny how she always Americanised his name and called him Sam. He didn't mind, he never corrected her. 'Did he say he booked his ticket?'

She looked straight at the road, 'No, he didn't'.

'Maybe it's too early. Maybe he'll get his ticket in the next week or so.'

She didn't reply and the silence between us was odd. I remembered last night's dream and again felt queasy.

The first time Sameer took me to his house was wonderful. Of course I had seen Janet and Uncle Kamal before at the club, so it was the house that was new. There was a policeman at the gate because Uncle Kamal was now Minister of Agriculture and their garden was much neater than ours. But I was more interested in the inside of the house - the way it looked and the way it smelled and its coolness. The colours were different from our house, more purple and orange. Then there were the pictures on the wall. One was rude because you could see the woman's breasts. One was a large black and white photo of Uncle Kamal when he was a student in Chicago. He looked so serious and handsome in a suit and a hat - just like in an old film. Everything in the house was from America, the furniture and the videotapes. Even the drink Sameer gave me, he said it was called Kool-Aid. His room had a poster of Malcolm X who I didn't know and Bob Marley who I did. On his desk were a pile of chemistry textbooks and a photo of me. In the sitting room we watched an early Soul Train on which The Supremes sang 'Baby Love' while Janet flicked through the pages of Ebony. I loved that magazine when I looked at it. 'You can take it, I'm all done with it,' Janet said. I took Ebony with me to school and showed it off to my friends. We had never seen a magazine like that before. Girls who looked like us but were glamorous, so obviously Western. I was proud of my future mother-in-law.

Janet turned the car left and we were suddenly bouncing down the dusty side street that led to the American Club. The club was at the end of the street; in front of it was a Christian cemetery. Janet parked facing the cemetery and I could see the headstones, a dusty statue of an angel. I felt confused. We were going to the Hilton. We couldn't be going to the cemetery. Maybe she was picking something up from the club? But she didn't say anything and got out of the car. I followed trying to think of something to say that wouldn't be rude. I couldn't say, 'I thought we were going to the Hilton' because that might be critical and complaining. Maybe I had misunderstood. Maybe we were going to the Hilton later. Maybe she would say something now about why she had changed her mind. She didn't.

We walked up the concrete path that led to the swimming pool. To the left was the tennis court, which on Saturday nights became a cinema. I was over-dressed for the club; I should have worn my denim skirt. I felt subdued because of that and because the club was full of memories. Here was where I had met Sameer and the first time he spoke to me, and the day he said, 'I dreamt of you last night' and the day I waited for him and he didn't come and all the times we drank grapefruit juice and shared paper plates of French Fries or sat by the pool his voice normal and bored asking the waiter 'So what's the special today' and his voice different and nice when he looked at me and said, 'Majda, do you want a Sloppy Joe?' And the day he said, 'My mom and dad want me to go to college in the States', and the day I gave him my diary to read, and afternoons watching him play tennis and the day we had our biggest quarrel because he said, 'This skirt is transparent don't wear it again.'

Janet chose a table by the pool. It was in the shade and she took off her sunglasses. She smiled at me and I smiled back, fighting disappointment. It was too late to mention the Hilton. Before she parked, I should have said innocently, 'I thought we were going to the Hilton!' Maybe I had misunderstood. My mother always tells me I only hear what I want to hear. I must have misunderstood Janet.

'Anyone that we know?' she scanned the pool and all the tables. I looked around too but my friends didn't come this time of day.

'There's Greta,' Janet said, nodding towards a large woman in a black swimsuit who was carefully coming out of the pool. Greta had big, beautiful blonde hair, cut short in a bob. Now it was a smooth wet sheet, clinging to her neck and shoulders. It made her head look small and her body huge.

Benjamin, the Southern waiter appeared. 'What will you have?' asked Janet. Unlike the Hilton there was no need for a menu here, we all knew it by heart.

'I don't know. What are you going to have?' I sounded sulky and felt ashamed. I sat up straight in my chair and opened my eyes wide so as to appear interested.

'What's the special?' she asked Benjamin.

'Chicken-in-the-basket.'

She raised her eyebrows, 'That sounds fun!'

I beamed back.

'Two specials, Benjamin,' she said, 'and I'll have an Iced Tea. Majda, what will you have to drink?'

'The same - Iced Tea,' I said even though I hated it.

Benjamin went away and we were quiet listening to the sounds of the club, watching the few who were swimming. I could hear the children from over the high wall that separated the club from St. Francis Primary School. The last time Sameer was here on holiday, we sometimes used to be quiet too and listen to the sounds of the school. I'd say to him, 'Tell me about America, tell me about your university.' He was glad he had gone. At first it had been his parents' idea and he didn't want to leave me, but now he said that studying in Chicago was great.

He came back different, he had changed, became more soft and more hard at the same time. He said sometimes he felt ashamed he was half-Sudanese and he wanted to throw that side of him away. 'Can you imagine how it feels, to be made up of two parts, one the richest most powerful country in the world and the other the poorest and weakest.' I said, 'You're just you, you're not made up of two parts. If you weren't genuinely Sudanese you wouldn't have got angry with me for wearing that see-through skirt.' He shrugged and said, 'That was last year, that was a long time ago.' So I wore it again, the day before he went back and he didn't complain.

'Janet!' It was Auntie Greta, making her way towards us in a billowing tie-dye dress, her damp hair combed away from her forehead. I stood up and kissed her. Her cheeks were cool and she smelt of chlorine. When she sat down she blocked my view of the pool.

'Did you enjoy your swim?' asked Janet.

'Oh yes. It's always nice and quiet this time of day'. Greta turned to me, 'And so when is the engagement party?'

I smiled, 'Next month, when Sameer comes for his holidays.' We were going to have a huge party at the Hilton, exchange rings, have a photographer as well as a video recording. When I thought of Sameer wearing a suit and me in my new evening dress, my stomach tightened with excitement.

'I don't understand this Sudanese custom of having official engagements,' said Janet to Greta, 'Why can't they just date like kids do in the States, they're so young!'

Greta shrugged, 'It's part of the Muslim culture.'

'I'm not that young,' I said, 'My mother was my age when she got married.'

They didn't say anything, just exchanged looks. For the first time it occurred to me that my mother was Sudanese and they were not, my mother was brought up as a Muslim and they were not.

'And when will you actually get married?' asked Greta.

This was a sore point. Sameer and I wanted to get married as soon as possible while both sets of parents insisted that he finish his studies first.

'Insha' Allah in a year or so,' I said. I wished people would stop asking me this question. It was more likely going to be in three year's time. It would be another decade then and anything could happen in between. Like last night's horrible dream: Sameer looking at me like I was nobody, like he couldn't remember me anymore. Sameer telling me he'd met someone else, someone American and prettier than me. It could happen, couldn't it? Uncle Kamal had been engaged to his cousin and then he went to study in Chicago and met Janet. Greta's husband had gone to study in Poland and came home with Greta. Maybe Sameer would meet someone too. There were no guarantees…if Allah didn't want us to get married, we wouldn't get married. It would be like today, thinking and dressing for the Hilton and ending up here.

'We're all looking forward to your wedding,' Greta said brightly.

I grimaced.

'Well, there's no hurry, they're still far too young,' said Janet, ' When they both graduate, insha' Allah.' She pronounced it as if it were all one word, inshallah. She said it in a way as if she was making fun.

Benjamin appeared with the Iced Teas and the chickens. He plonked a napkin in front of me that was more grey than white. The knife and fork had stains that I rubbed away with my fingers. Where was I now and where was the Hilton?

'Can you get me ketchup, please', I said to Benjamin. The club made it's own ketchup. It was cheaper than the imported Heinz and tasted more tomatoey.

'Have something, Greta'; Janet raised her hand to detain Benjamin.

'I'll just have a Pepsi'.

I ate my chicken and listened to them talk. Janet ate her chicken with her hand and so I did too. I liked listening to them: all the foreign wives' gossip. Many of the American Club members were foreign wives married to Sudanese men. Many like Sameer had foreign mothers. I was a rare exception, a hundred percent Sudanese. For me foreignness was like a dress I put on, it was not in my blood. Greta didn't have any children. When Greta first came to Khartoum, she had lived next door to Janet and Janet had helped her settle in. Now Greta said something funny about diets and I laughed. Janet smiled and wiped her mouth with her napkin. She was so dainty next to her loud, hearty friend.

'I have something to show you,' said Greta looking at me, 'this is me and Janet when I first came to Khartoum nineteen years ago. Look how thin I was!' From her handbag, she took out a black and white photo. She put it in front of me and Janet leaned over to look. In the photo Greta was unrecognisable, slim and with long flowing blonde hair. And Janet looked exactly like the most beautiful of The Supremes, her hair high on her head. She was holding Sameer on her lap. He was the most gorgeous, gorgeous baby; smiling and bald, dimpled and fat. I couldn't help it, it came out in a whine, 'Aah, I want to have a baby like that.'

'Not till my son graduates, honey,' said Janet taking away the photo from me and giving it back to Greta. 'I'm in NO hurry to be a grandma!'

I stared at the place on the table where the photo had been. Greta patted my arm. 'Insha' Allah you'll have lots of babies, Majda,' she said, her eyes soft and grey. She put the photo back in her handbag and said, 'Well, I'd better be off now.'

I watched her as she walked away, dwarfing Benjamin who crossed her path. I said to Janet, 'Auntie Greta looked so beautiful when she was young.' It was as if I could still see the photograph.

'Those were actually hard years for Greta,' Janet said gesturing to Benjamin to get the bill. 'She kept having one miscarriage after the other. She went all the way to London and had all sorts of treatment with a doctor in Harley Street but it was no use. They're loaded but there are some things money can't buy.'

'Is there a way of being sure that when ….if … whether someone can have a baby or not…?'

'Not unless you start trying, no.'

'So maybe, just maybe,' I croaked, 'Sameer and I won't ever …ever be able to have any babies?'

'Oh for God's sake, Majda, let the future take care of itself!'

'I'm sorry,' I mumbled. It seemed the right thing to say because I had annoyed her and made her raise her voice.

'Look,' she said, her voice was low but her eyes shrewd and knowing. 'You're very young. You'll change as you get older, you'll see things differently. Maybe you'll even change your mind about Sam…'

'No, never,' I interrupted but she went on.

'Or maybe you'll decide you don't want to get married at all.' She raised both her hands. 'There are all sorts of possibilities. Why, yesterday on the phone, Sam was saying he might not be able to make it to the engagement next month! He's changed, Majda, he's been thinking things over. Personally I think he's far too young to commit himself but that's something you two will have to talk over.'

I was again in my bad dream. The sick fear. He'd met someone else. Another girl, American and prettier than me.

She looked away from me, at the club. She sounded dreamy like she was talking to herself. 'There are so many fresh opportunities for him there. To come back here, to tie himself to Sudan, would be a step backward.'

I strained to understand, to get it right this time, not to hear Hilton and end up in the club.

She looked at me and laughed. 'Oh don't you dare start crying here in front of everyone!' She touched my cheek and made her voice sweet. 'Come on now, finish your drink and then I can drive you home.'

I gulped the rest of my Iced Tea and coughed. It was diluted and more horrible because of the melted ice.

About the author:

Leila Aboulela was born in Cairo and spent the early years of her life in Sudan, attending both school and university in Khartoum. She is an internationally acclaimed, award-winning writer and has had her work translated into twelve languages.

O' HALFA
By Miada Ahmed Akasha

"Life is naught but a road and a home."

Home… how the heart aches for you. Spilled tears of generations do not even begin to describe the longing. Where would I have played with the neighbours down the street? When would I have had my first dive in the cool waters of the Nile? Which tree would I have climbed and divulged myself on its fruits? Who would be the first aunt to scold me for climbing trees and swimming late? How would the air taste? What would the sounds feel?

Would I – we – still be feeling this sense of estrangement and deracination?

Home… is now several miles below the water, forever dormant in a deep blue grave, and we are sentenced to eternal exile.

Halfa's beauty was in its openness, its nature, its Geography. Picturesque, it lay cosily amidst valleys of greenery. Miles upon miles of palm and fruit trees stretched with resplendence as far as the eye can see. Standing on a knoll gives a view of a stretched emerald horizon. Its land is perfect for arable farming and seasonally gets flooded by the Nile's riches. Crops ranging from wheat to fruit; the people of Halfa knew no hunger. The Nile River ruled the land; beside irrigation, people used it for transport, whether to travel further along the river or across it, since the villages were spread on both banks. People used it for drinking, washing, cooking. Moreover, it was an important part of ceremonies and sacred rituals; a bride and her groom, for instance, must rinse their faces at the Nile's bank together. Such was the significance of the Nile River that every child by the age of four knew how to swim.

Halfa's beauty was in its History. A several thousand year old civilization has flourished and thrived on its sands. Ancient pharaohs, both men and women, ruled the kingdoms with their pyramids and their gold which was in such abundance the prisoners cuffs were made of it.

Halfa's beauty was in its language. Unique to its people, the language spoken is called Nubian, handed down from the glorious Nubian ancestors. This language is gender-neutral in nouns and pronouns, due to the fact that Nubians saw men and women as equals.

Halfa's beauty was in its air, its water, its earth.

And now its beauty is just a memory of past splendour and magnificence gone too soon.

And who remembers but us? The books – their pages decay with time. The songs – they will be forgotten. The maps – they no longer hold its name; where it once was with all its majesty is now labelled a lake, a vast "nothing". Our memories – they will fade until one day we will have no ability to recall them. The present generation – they only have frequently retold nostalgic tales, lent stories and their imaginations.

EXODUS

The dark one-way train, on its journey to leave but to never return… that is what stood out the most in the people's memory.

On the station the mood was desolate and morose. Whether silently crying or wailing hopelessly, families were divided between those going to the New Halfa and those who are settling with moving to the higher grounds nearby. They were caught between two evils: a desolate desert or the uninhabitable lands.

Ahmed didn't understand why Khalid was leaving. 'My mom needs the hospital, Ahmed,' Khalid explained.

'She can give birth here,' Ahmed said back.

'There are no hospitals or doctors here. There is nothing here. I don't even know why you're staying. You are holding on to nothing.'

'This is my home – OUR home. It shouldn't be abandoned. You'll wish you could come back.'

A LAND THAT ONCE WAS: Ahmed's story/ Old Halfa

Those who abandoned the land felt that desperately holding on to what is left – which is nothing – is desperate and fruitless. They were right.

The past years have been the worst years of my life, and if I stay, I know that only worse is yet to come. Everything is a struggle. There were no schools or facilities. The only schools available were at nearby villages. Going there was travelling daily. The winters were the toughest. I remember early morning, walking in the dark to my school, alongside many children, in the cold, will-less and broken.

My sister, like many others, gave up going to school altogether. The walk was long and tedious. And the schools themselves were poorly equipped: the sand was our ground and the sky was our ceiling.

As the water over our drowned home rises, so are we forced to continue ascending the highlands. And as we feel that the winter cannot get any colder, we get proven wrong with our ascent. No heat, no electricity, no hospitals... death was imminent and suffocating.

But the most pain came whenever we looked north-west and saw the lake; the lake that was our death sentence, the killer of our world, the indigo catacomb. A permanent reminder as wide and as deep as despair.

I should have left. I should have left.

A LAND THAT WILL NEVER BECOME: Khalid's story/ New Halfa

What is this place? I always ask myself that question. What is this place that is posing as my home? This will never be Halfa. This dry desert as far as the eye can see will never be the heaven that I came from.

If all of us were permanently sentenced to eternal depression, my uncle I think took it the worst. Not long after we settled he started collecting wood and constructing something in front of his house. Passersby would ask him what he was building and he would always reply vaguely: 'If you haven't forgotten where you were from, you would know.'

Several months later of solo toil, it became a yacht, a big boat with the highest sail I have ever seen, just like the ones back home, ready to voyage the Nile. But where is it? Where is the Nile? Where is the Queen of the Land? Where is the vein of our lives?

And so sat my uncle's boat, awkwardly, miserably on dry land, neither cruising nor gliding, stuck ever so rigidly with no glory, just a memory of paradise.

Anyone who saw the glorious yacht wept. And my uncle, my uncle's life was consumed with it. He would sit facing it for hours on end. It wore him away too. Slowly, it ate him; he never talked, rarely ate, forgot to live.

Until one cold winter we found him dead, sitting on his chair facing the yacht. Nobody needed to ask why he died. Even I with my young age knew that Misery and Homesickness kill.

My sister's, with whom my mom was pregnant during the Exodus, first question after learning to speak was, 'What is that?', pointing at the boat.

'That is our home,' I had replied to her, thankful that my uncle died before hearing this question. Just like that, the new generation had hurt me in an unimaginable way. How could I begin to explain home to her? How could I show her?

I wish I never left, I wish I never left.

By: Miada Ahmed Akasha - A Wadi Halfa Immigrant

This story is inspired by the people of Halfa including Manar Tofik, who adored the River Nile, and Ahmed Akasha, the little Ahmed who felt that home should not be abandoned.

About the author:

I wasn't born in Sudan but I was lucky enough to go there yearly and even studied University there. I'm a Pharmacist but I've had a passion for writing ever since I was little. I'm an avid reader, a movie buff, an eclectic listener, future world traveller, nostalgic but optimistic, and either a dancer or a rhythm butcher.

A LETTER TO KHARTOUM
by Rund Al-Arabi

At midnight

the car breaks the silence of Khartoum town with its tired tyres as I watch the blinking red lights while humming the wishes of a goodnight to the old buildings of downtown Khartoum that I'm sure my soul loved and lost while running around its crowded alleys, goodnight to the crickets who circled my nights with symphonies, shared with me my moments of solitude as the flashing lights of cars coloured the walls of my dark room like a cinema screen. Goodnight, to the man I've wholeheartedly loved and shared the same sky with, but never the destiny.

To my family, loved ones who are scattered like broken glass over the world's map whom I can't wish a goodnight because they may have just woken up, goodnight to you, the one stuck in the middle
between your country that spits out your dreams and another that only craves for your sweat.

As I pass by the Nile watching the little waves sculpting the shape of little black pyramids I send a goodnight to Sittat Al-shai who serve their hopes on cups of coffee, sugar spoonfuls of a better future for their kids. To the University of Khartoum, the study sheets, burning tests molded by the dandurmas we used to pick up on our way home.

Goodnight to Fatima Al-samha, Al-ghool, Shilail, Toor Al-lail and every character whose tales my brother used to spook us with when the lights cut off.

Goodnight to the moon, you hid behind the sun so we couldn't see you, but followed me wherever I went just like my thoughts of him.

To Khartoum, the song that we often happen to sing out of tune.

Goodnight to the city, the village, the traces of a capital and the leftovers of a country Khartoum, Love.

About the author:

Rund Mohammed Al-Arabi is a 21 year old girl who lives in Sudan, majored in French and Linguistics. She tries to keep the thoughts to herself but her fingers always tend to disobey.

Illustration by Hussein Merghani

SUDAN
by Abdul-Rahman Bashir Ali

Sudan
I love her as a mother loves its child
Unconditionally, blindly, absolute-
The odour she produces is so sweet
So unique
But it hurts me to see her suffering
To witness all she goes through
Screaming in pain
Injected with poverty
Coughing in pollution
Self-harming
Civil war and split into two
Yet she'll come through stronger.

I love her because she's developing just as I am
Trying to become a better land, and I, a better man
Each grain of sand holds its own weight
Competing against each passing day
The complexity of faces all with a different story to tell
The art of conversation still boding well
Thus she is stripped.

Its children seeking higher learning
With scuffed feet;
Signs of walking throughout the seasons
Throughout the heat
But education is for the smart
And smart we must be
Sacrifice everything you can to set your mind free
A vision engraved deep within
Set by family name therefore failure is not an option
Failure does not exist.

Sudan's a land that needs trade not aid
If you stand back you'll realize that hand-outs are great
Until the hand moves away – Who will then feed you?
Sudan can stand on its own two
She boasts the beautiful Nile
Earth that's fertile
With climates of all types-
Hard working genes
People looking for a means
The sweetest of coffee beans-
A land full of history, honour and pride.

Emerge from the myth and drown in research
Get lost in the Sahara desert reading Ibrahim Salman
And you'll find that she's sentimental in value
Motherland is her name – poor but rich
Not free from pain.
Divided by thoughts
Separated by courts
And, instead of joining forces to force out famine
She loiters in loneliness
Slowly torn in two
A divided nation
A broken home
A tug of war that's ended numb
A new map drawing
New face, but still the same problems.
A drop of oil below the soil-
Suffocates the children's growth
For, what is it worth if you lose the value of its earth.
Nothing.

With the youth relying on older generations to tell tales of a nation we once were
That once stood
Brings together a crowd-
A cool sunset
Warm memories and Polaroid pictures have the audience in awe
As we're lost in description
And in that brief moment
With my eyes drawn closed
I'm taken to a place where I can escape the everyday struggle and lies
The corruption, protests and fights
The child soldiers emptying clips of rounds
Not understanding their consequences
Not understanding the cries.

So I take my place and sit patiently, ever eager to hear tales
Real life fantasies at an arm's length-
I try to grab on, as he begins to talk about a dignified age
The Nile and golden sand
People who feed empty hands
How Africa's heart, was found in Sudan-
Where you'll be greeted with love
Emotions and hugs
Traditions that spur
Conditions to unnerve
A hidden gem unearthed
Food with taste
Conversations in face
People who embrace

And with time to spare
Who offer an ear – and love to care
Bright colours – red, white and gold
A weekly wedding, the perfect setting
Those working on ships, who take long trips
Working hard to bring their fortunes home
So much to learn
And a promise that when you leave
they'll be waiting on your return
Perfectly picturing the image he paints
I can feel its warmth and hear the birds sing
Morning tea and conversing
I can walk up to a date tree and pluck its sweetness
And smell flavours of food beyond description
I can vividly hear him speak, as I'm lost so deep in description
The sound of the azhan – left, right, both behind and before me
As people close their stalls and head towards the house of God
In white robes and football tops
Wishing I lived his day and age, I no longer want to open my eyes to face today.

He pauses
With his chin resting on his hands
Held up by his walking stick that's placed into the ground.
No one dares to speak
As my eyes stay focused-
On a frail figure, soft natured, wrinkled skin-
That has a tale for each one of his lines
Dressed in a thin white cloth, that's adopted the colour of dust
The colour of Sudan
With the hills itching for more
Index to the sky
He leaves with advice…

You can't re-write history
Nor can you predict the future
Pick up a book now
Tomorrow you're a teacher
Let struggle be the basis of your success
Look at the countries around us trying to progress
Let opportunity motivate you more and money less
Laugh in the face of stress
Then, remember the tired look your parents possessed
Tighten the grip on your ambitions
Be all you can be – to raise the country up off its knees
Close your eyes and believe
Don't be chased by your nightmares – for not living your dreams
Believe in hope and in turn hope will grow
Pray for needs-

But at the same time water your seeds
Know that today's children are nurtured
So tomorrow we survive
It's on you to stand up and make things right
It's on you to stand up and make peace unite
If the Nile hasn't split..
Then why must its people fight?

About the author:

My name is Abdul-Rahman Bashir. I was born and raised in London with parents originating from Dongola, north of Khartoum. I began writing poetry as a form of passing time, but very soon came to realise that poetry was a means of creating beauty and art from words.

SANDS OF WONDER
by Zainab Aljundi

A sand storm rises in the deep African Desert; it lifts up each sand particle into the air entranced in a spell. The particles move in unified unison as though life has been breathed into a large being. With each breath the beast takes it soars through the air like a mighty sword of glass.

As the beast takes the deepest of breaths it's particles unleash, entwining and unravelling in a celebratory dance of life, a seamless dance of wonder.

This graceful mountainous moving piece of art entrances the eyes, but beware stepping in to join the dance, for the unsheathed blades will tear your limbs apart.

As the night slips away and the darkness crawls back into hiding, fearing the blood red streaks of sunrise seeping through, the beast takes its last breath and lays to rest. Although, not for long.

About the author:

A goofy 28 year-old preschool teacher. My best pieces were not something I sat and thought about, they just "came" to me. Inspiration sometimes even woke me up and words just poured onto the paper, writing in the dark, imagine how fun encrypting that in the morning was.

WHO IS SHE?
by Eva Andrew

She was a graceful dove, her pulchritude a phantom draped in a willowy demeanor, embedded in a picturesque entity. She held the type of beauty that couldn't even be delineated by the best image painter, the type of beauty that couldn't even be expressed in the most scenic of languages, the type of beauty that made Mother Nature suspire with envy. She was known for her heart, a confluence that harbored heaven's tears, compiling them in a single being that quenched the thirstiest of men, a being that extended from the palaces of the richest to the gutters of the poorest, a being that enveloped the land around it in wealth worth more than a mount of gold, a being that provided refuge for everything marine, a being that enwrapped everything within her to paragon, a being that made its roars heard even to the deaf, a river that satisfied not only her, but her siblings likewise.

She was timeless; basking in a state of perpetual bliss, her ideality worked wonders. She was the option that shouldn't have been chosen, her love a lethal weapon to anyone that chose to act presumptuously against her will. She was a savage lover that could never be stopped, her heart a missile aimed at her most ardent supporters. She was a vehement guardian of her dignity, a monster that put an end to anyone that posed a threat. She demanded to be loved, her heart a fiery fireplace, yet, oddly enough, she brought about destruction to anyone who could possibly rekindle the flame of affection in her; it was almost as though she put up a heaven with all its joys and pleasures, only to entice people and later reveal flames so fervid, they could be none other than Satan's. But they still loved her, they were addicted to the pain; whether it was the heat she brought to every room, or the dust her feet carried everywhere, something about her was remarkably bewitching, and they just couldn't let go; it was like you couldn't hate her even if you tried to – her beauty was a culture of its own. Some left, but they came back eventually, unable to ignore the scars she left imprinted on their hearts, the marks she had them tattooed with; after all, one surely cannot let go of their culture any more than a baby bird can let go of its mother.

Her soul's inhabitants were as dark as the graves their ancestors lay in, with intentions as pure as a child's sopor, clothing with more colors than a peacock's behind, noses that extended from the north end to the south, lips as full as a flood is of water, voices breathing honeyed words with each diction, spirits much like the moon with its meek shine – silvery and modulated to her friends, intensely venomous to her foes. They were fierce fighters, messengers of death to their hostiles; their bodies were sturdy, their rugged strength clearly marked by the mass of muscle they called body parts. Yet there were still those who were elegantly stunning, their shapely bodies the ideal definition of a woman. It seemed, however, that her soul wasn't where one would choose to live had they had the option; it was what people needed, but not what they wanted, it was what was available, but not what they were after, it was enough, but not comfortably adequate. How is it that she allowed some to live amply, basking in her riches, yet most were left to rot in the streets with no more than a slice of bread to survive on? How is it that she allowed the creation of such a barrier between the elite and the common masses?

She wore diamonds on her neck that gleamed with dreamlike enchantment, gracefully draped upon her swart skin; they swayed in a synchronized velvety manner from side to side with each stroke, like a dandelion's bristles on a windy morning. Her collarbones protruded in a manner that would've driven even the bravest of men away; so frightening, yet so beautifully fascinating, she was the human encompassment of surrealism. Her arms were bony figures trying to use human skin to disguise their ghastliness, yet there was something about them; maybe it was their luminescent glow, maybe it was the bumps you encountered as you travelled from her wrist to her elbow to her shoulder, maybe it was all of the little, barely-there blemishes that ran along the curves of her bones like pebbles in a dark, misty river. Her cheekbones were mesmerizing, jutting out of her hollow cheeks in a matter as serene as the night skies before a storm, seemingly unapparent but only so in preparation of great turbulence. Emaciation had never draped itself so beautifully.

History is an amazingly stunning thing, but too bad we had to live in the present; they say that each minute counted, that each day brought about change, which meant that two decades would bring about a hurricane of alteration. But there was something unmistakably wrong; she had bruises as dark as the bottom of a well staining her immaculate body, her face now holding a path engraved by the sleepless nights spent weeping, waiting for the knight that was never showing up. Her sunken eyes squalled frustration, shedding tears hoping that her saviour would be nearby. Her once luscious curls were now unbowed stalks of weathering straw, as voluminous as the depth of snow on a hot summer day. She walked with a hobble, moving flaccidly from side to side as she struggled to find her balance, oblivious to the fact that the blind cannot be made to see, the dumb cannot be made to speak, and the crippled cannot be made to walk. Her once full lips now bled a colour as red as the roses she once grew in the garden that was her mind, with cracks on what was left – the broken windows to her now empty soul. It seemed the loss of her child, the separation of their two bound souls, had taken its toll; this did not resemble anything she had ever been through before – the torment was beyond human comprehension. It was the separation of intertwined souls, the division of conjoined twins, the disjoining of a body part.

She thought she had a secret, but only, it was no longer a secret; she could try to hide her brokenness, but that was about as useful as trying to hide a ship amidst sea from an approaching blizzard. The loss of their child had a greater toll on her husband, leaving him in a state of melancholia that used rage to express itself. Her once elated rapture turned into an abusive relationship, one that stripped her of her assets, one that detained her beauty in a cell hidden so far down, it seemed impossible that such a desolate location were even to exist; she was a young rosebud forced into a toxic marriage, her spouse a destructive force that orphaned her of everything she once loved. Her siblings weren't too fond of this husband of hers, but nothing could be done about it, for they were as damaged as she was; after all, a bleeding man surely cannot tend to another's cuts without tending to his own first, can he? She often contemplated ways of escaping what seemed like eternal doom, her train of thought almost always leading to the key that required her to gain enough courage to stand up for herself; she had to be her own knight in shining armour, she had to be her own salvation, she had to be both the warrior and the sword in the upcoming war.

What never failed to amaze people is that after all of the anguish, after all of the walking through bushes' spines, after tending to more bullet wounds than she could count, she still had hope; she longed for days when she would finally recover, believing that there actually was an end to the agony, and that maybe her child would finally come back home. There is no denying that it took courage to keep walking the walk of shame, to keep pulling out the thorns infixed in her by her supposed lover, to keep breathing despite the disapproval of her lungs, to keep reciting the rhapsody her partner warned her against, to keep herself from pulling the trigger she had aimed at her own head, but it just wasn't enough. The courage to stand up to him and break the constraints he had her tied with hadn't been imbedded in her just yet; he still controlled her every move, bringing her independent individualism to an all time low. But she was going to keep walking that boulevard of broken hearts, she was going to keep anticipating the return of their long-lost child, she was going to keep allowing her wounds to heal. She was powerful, yet tremendously weak; she was trying to hold herself together, but kept falling apart as each day passed; she was clinging on to life so dearly, but her body chose to let go; she was the Sudan.

About the author:

Eva Andrew is a sixteen year old Bulgarian residing in Sudan. She is currently in the eleventh grade, completing her final year in high school. In her spare time, she enjoys painting, cooking and doing bad impressions of her friends and family.

LIFE ON RENT
by Ayuel Atem

Life on Rent.
I live in this place, not my own.
it's the only home I've ever known,
it owns the memory of me grown.
it shall see the seeds that I've sown.

I digress, this place is not a home,
it is where I rest when troubles come.
it may not seem like much to some,
I've grown to love it during my time.

it has seen storms and endless calm.
it bears the mark of my silent psalms.
of the time I was under the soldiers Palm.
And the sweet allure of my mother's charm

About the author:

My name is Ayuel Atem and I am a law student at Moi University in Kenya. I'm South Sudanese in origin - Dinka. I was born in Cairo, Egypt but lived most of my life in Kenya.

A DECADE'S JOURNEY IN SUDAN
By Bhaskar Chakravorti

Ten years ago, moving to Sudan brought up appalling Western media images of a country ravaged by war, extreme heat and dust, and primitive in its development. And then came the surprise. After an initial period of settling in, looking for fellow Indians and foods and spices, I learned that this country, in which I would spend the next ten years, was very different from the images that were projected of it. I learned of ancient historical trade ties of spice, gold and silk between the Meroe kingdom and Indian traders who used the Red Sea as a shipping route, and I learned that the Sudanese people themselves were friendly, safe, honest, but slightly laid back!

Historians have traced indications of direct contact between India and the Kingdom of Kush - Napata and Meroe (750 BC to 300 AD). Today there are about 2000 persons in the Indian community spread all over Sudan. The first Indian trader from this community arrived in Suakin in 1856. The first Sudanese Parliamentary elections in 1953 were conducted by Sukumar Sen, India's Chief Election Commissioner (the Sudanese Election Commission, formed in 1957, drew heavily on Indian election literature and laws).

In April 1955 there was a Sudanese delegation at Bandung (Indonesia) to attend the Conference of Africa and Asia. Since Sudan was still not independent and did not have a national flag yet, India's first Prime Minister Jawaharlal Nehru wrote out Sudan on his white handkerchief and created a flag for Sudan. A building in the Military College in India is named 'Sudan Block' as a memorial for the Indian army who fought for the British in World War II in Sudan.

My Sudanese friends keep telling me that India has made its mark as a major player in global economy, as a nuclear power nation with technological advancements in the IT software and pharmaceuticals sectors. Hindi films are very popular and have made their presence felt in the salons of almost every household. Above all, the most respected Indian personality in Sudan is Mahatma Gandhi. Mahatma Gandhi had stopped over in Port Sudan in 1935 on his way to England.

Coming back to my experience in Sudan, I found the traffic was on the wrong side of the road! India, being a British colony, drove on the left side of the road and that is what I did. But help was at hand in the form of Mohammed El Hassan who taught me to drive the 'right' way in Sudan, and I am so used to it now that in India I now decline from driving during my vacations as that is now the 'wrong side' of the road! Mohammed El Hassan now works with me and is an Indophile. He has visited India on a number of occasions and looks forward to many more.

Bashir Ahmed Bashir was my Arabic tutor when I arrived. He was sincere, hardworking and dynamic. I recommended this young man, who used to work in a bagala, for a job in an NGO where the Manager was a friend. Bashir was sent to Geneina in Darfur where he did a sterling job. He later joined the UN, and as part of his job, he has already visited Geneva.

Moez El Sheikh had dreams to be spun on celluloid – this young filmmaker was connected to the Department of Communication Sciences. I recommended him to the Embassy of India for the ITEC programme and he was sent to India with a scholarship for a technical course.

Dr. Anwar Ahmed Osman is an Astronomer par excellence and my current Arabic tutor. He teaches me Arabic and I teach him Marketing. I created a marketing plan for an exhibition on Space and Astronomy, which ran for many months at the Green Yard. I want to see him fulfil his dream of having a planetarium in Khartoum and perhaps with the help of the Ministries of both countries, visit planetariums in Mumbai and Kolkata for further ideas.

My constant travel companion is my camera and is a record keeper of my time here. I have travelled to Port Sudan, Erkaweit, Merowe, Kareema, Naga, Bajrawiya, Atbara, Wad Madani and El Damazin; social utilities such as Facebook, Blogs, Twitter, and so on, have informed my friends and acquaintants of the many wonders of this land, from the ancient brick pyramids at Kareema to the site at Naga which the UN has declared of great international historical importance because of its antiquity and the influence it had on the Egyptian civilization. Prior to the partition I also visited Juba to look for marketing opportunities there.

My photographic coverage of medical doctors and the medical conferences, as well as pharmacists, has often brought a smile on their lips when I have presented them with their photographs.

I believe in using all the new technology and social media available, and like all marketing men, I maintain an extensive mailing list through which I have been able to provide employment opportunities or business deals to some people.

While the people of Sudan are open, friendly and good, I have always felt that customer relations/support needed improvement. To this effect I have led workshops on training new employees in soft business skills and knowledge of customers in action.

As I work for a pharmaceutical company, I share medical updates via email with my list of doctors many of whom appreciate this electronic update. I also cover the medical conferences, Indian community and other topics of interest for the English Daily in Khartoum – Sudan Vision. The weblink is posted to my Facebook page so my world outside Sudan is aware of what is happening here.

I will end with an old West African proverb- 'If you want to go quickly, go alone. If you want to go far, go together.' I would like to go far in my journey in Sudan with my friends here and Inshallah as we say here: 'Experience is a strong walking stick' and with that walking stick I would like to live the rest of my days here.

About the author:

Bhaskar grew up as a child in Darjeeling. He graduated from Presidency College and obtained an MBA from the University of Calcutta. His career in Pharmaceutical Marketing took him to the smallest villages and biggest cities of India. Having spent more than ten years in Sudan he has grown to love the country.

RE-CREATING EDEN
by Zoe Troy Cormack

We were on our way to Kuajok. The voice of John Garang, South Sudan's greatest martyr, filled our white Land Cruiser. The lady next to me laughed and cheered as she listened. Her hand, manicured, gripped the door handle to steady herself. We were hurtling along a wide rough road; ricocheting off the seats and each other. The voice filtered out of the speakers into the cool, air-conditioned car

'Many people will be surprised that in the Bible, in the Old Testament, the Sudan was part of the Garden of Eden…'

The others must have heard this speech a thousand times before. Six years earlier, it was delivered in Nairobi at the signing of a peace deal that ended the 23-year civil war, which had, ultimately, torn Sudan apart. The canny voice explained how the Old Testament describes the four rivers that watered Eden, then tells how these rivers - Pessian, Gihon, Tigris and the Euphrates - are the ones that water the modern country of Sudan

'So the Garden of Eden was not a small vegetable garden. It was a vast piece of territory. My own village happens to be just east of the Nile. So I fall in the Garden of Eden.'

This was an Eden shattered and shaken. Now the politicians were putting it back together again. That was the claim and the hope.

Kuajok is a long way from anywhere most people have heard of, two days drive from South Sudan's capital city, Juba. It's an island of high ground in a seasonal swamp. It's the capital of Warrap State and five years ago it barely existed. It's run by women – by that I mean the local government has a strong female elite – a woman Governor and a number of female Ministers and MPs. These women meant a lot to me, because I moved in with one of them – the lady in the Land Cruiser - for nine months while I did my doctoral research. Most aid workers I met in Kuajok did not think it was habitable; no 24-hour power; no Internet; no swimming pool.

Our journey began in a town called Wau. I was loaded into the back of a car, squeezed in between my host and a former Commissioner. To my left the Honerable Adut Madut Akec, MP: this daughter of a rotund Dinka veterinarian had an immaculate hair cut, a skirt suit and a gap between her two front teeth. The Commissioner to my right had lost his leg in the late 1980s, fighting for the Southern rebel movement at the border with Ethiopia. Adut's father was famous in the 1950s and 1960s for his large belly, and insistence on calling passers by into his house in Gogrial to fill up on food if they looked hungry. Adut had imbibed her father's sense of hospitality. I was being fussed over, given biscuits and water. Later that night I would eat three dinners.

Leaving Wau we drove past crumbling colonial buildings, it was a glimpse of old Sudan, ex-Sudan, the historic Sudan, which had ceased to exist exactly three months and twelve days earlier. Wau had been a government garrison during the last war. Although bitterly divided and steeped in suspicion, it offered a relative safety in the middle of the active fighting that raged in the countryside. Thousands of people fled here. Despite years of neglect the buildings in the town are intact, but they bear the wounds of war and carry the memories of them. A university lecturer had taken me to visit the old Catholic Church and he had pointed out its walls covered in children's drawings: guns, soldiers and warplanes.

We passed dilapidated shacks, remnants of shelters hurriedly built by people who had run here to escape from the violence in the places we were now driving toward. We crossed over the old barracks, over the railway line and through a small forest of mango trees on the outer rim of the semi-urbanity. A piece of cool shade before the heat of the long road. A few months later I was told by a Sudan People's Liberation Army commander that he had ordered his troops to plant these mangos when their battalion was stationed outside of the town, twenty years before. Armies sometimes create beautiful things.

The end of the war had meant many changes. The transformation of this tiny village was one of them. Kuajok had only become a place on the map when it was made a mission station in the 1920s. After John Garang's peace agreement, its course changed and it was made the capital of a state. Then Garang himself died in a helicopter accident in 2005 and South Sudan steered towards Independence. There is a lot of talk about what could be. But in Kuajok, the narrative of a new South Sudan doesn't only exist on the lips of the politicians; it is being built with the fabric of the town itself.

Drive into Kuajok from the South, as we did, you find yourself first in the old part of town. The Catholic missionaries built a church and a school here and settled in to teach (and convert) the local Dinka people. The church is still standing. It was built in 1924 and it could well be the oldest building in South Sudan that is still used as it was originally intended. This little place left a big mark on the country. Many of today's leaders in South Sudan, including the president, Salva Kiir, came here to go to school. Father Nebel, an Austrian missionary in Kuajok, was the first person to write the Dinka language. He produced a dictionary and some grammar guidelines, wrote little passages in Dinka that are still taught to schoolchildren. On my second day in Kuajok I went to see the Church. It was the only part of town I had seen mentioned in any history books. I was shown around by the current parish priest, Father Ariath. Not fat, exactly, but well looked after. Something about his feet, which seemed too big for his body, gave him a reassuring posture. He leans over you, leans in to talk.

During the last civil war, the Church was used as military barracks, the roof was destroyed, the paintwork and the interior washed away by rain. The local Catholic diocese has since restored it, they have replaced the iron roof, and they have repainted the walls. Discovering that I was trying to learn the Dinka language, Father Ariath leaned over and repeated one of the Austrian missionary's passages to me:

Yon Nhialic Kuajok,	Kuajok Church
Adit ku Dheŋ apɛi	Is big and very beautiful!
Agep aci giit pany kɔu,	Palm trees are on the walls
Aci kum nhom yar weeth,	It is covered with iron sheeting
Nhialic a acieŋ cak kɔc	God created people
Kɔc path aa Nhialic rɔɔk	Good people pray to God

I looked up to crisp newly painted palm trees on bright white walls and realized they were the same palms. The salvaged church had been made to match an image in a children's poem.

Many of the shacks that we had seen on our journey from Wau belonged to people displaced from around Kuajok in the civil war. Kuajok was in the wrong place during the 1990s. A small village on the road between strategically important and embattled towns, it was marched over and over by soldiers. They used the church as a base; that is how it lost its roof. Kuajok is close to the railway line from the north, the train link brought hostile militia loyal to the Sudanese Government down, close to where people lived. It was part of the way this war was fought. In 1995, these militias brought indelible horror. They swept through the area, looting cattle and killing people. The violence has lingered, it can't quite be erased. Corpses were flung into wells and barely covered. There is one water grave in what is now the police station. The past in Kuajok is still lurking, quite literally, just below the surface.

In the years that followed, most of the late 1990s, people were too afraid to plant crops; the militia had taken cattle; there was not enough food. Eventually the people in Kuajok had no choice but to cross the nearby River Jur to seeming safety, to a place called Ajiep where the UN and aid workers had come with donated food. But swathes of exhausted people arrived and there was not enough donated food to go around. There was naiveté, panic and mis-management. After reaching presumed safety, people died. The rates of death here were galling, each day, over 100 of the 17,500 people who had fled here succumbed. You only have to dig a little to find this history. Ask a beggar in the market: in the days of Ajiep his father had taken it upon himself to dig graves for the dead. The intensity of the physical labour, for a man already malnourished, was too much and he died himself. His son, left without a mother or father, now begs for food. There is a woman who lost her mind after her family was killed in front of her, she rambles and accosts passers by as they do their shopping. They are the physical remains of war.

One of the first things I was told when I got to Kuajok was that 'this place used to be a forest', this place was wild, but now it is tame. Leading to the church, along a mud road lined with mango trees, are ramshackle houses, made of mud and salvaged parts of old brick buildings. This is the oldest part of town: 'Kuajokdit'. It's where all the MPs and ministers moved to when Kuajok became the state capital. There was nowhere else for them to live. Now they have moved on, into the wider streets and new bricks of the up and coming, well to do suburbs. The new Kuajok is a grid vision of modernity and order. The elite have built grand and gated houses next to traditional round huts with conical roofs. The new poor of Kuajok have settled into the old houses. Some of the women that live in these abandoned homes walk into town carrying bundles of grass on their heads. They sell them in the market; one bundle will bring ten South Sudanese pounds. Sell two bundles and you can buy a tin of sorghum grain, take it home, pound and grind it, boil it with water and the thick plain porridge stretches to one meal for a family.

Even when they have built a grand new house, people still live and even sleep outside. It's too hot in South Sudan to be inside. There is no public electricity; very few have the generators and fuel needed to cool themselves down with air conditioning. These bright houses are for looking, not living. Kuajok is still being built and rebuilt and it doesn't matter. The houses are a reminder that people want to invest here. Even the President is building here: his house, on the road that comes from Wau, hides behind an imposing concrete wall. Every time I passed I could see this wall constantly being tended, painted and repainted white because the rain and the wind washed away the poor quality paint that is still all anyone can buy in the market. Beyond the wall, the house is half constructed. Between gorges of mud, where women in old clothes and plastic shoes carefully pick their way, a villa with watchtowers rises.

For a few months, I spent every evening sitting outside a construction site in Adut's compound, as her new house slowly rose too. At some point her niece would climb over rubble to bring us our food on a big metal tray and water to wash our hands. Adut's life had slotted itself in to the gaps in the building work. An initial flurry of work on the house had died down while more money was saved up. The work lingered on and I frequently reassured Adut that this is a fact of life all over the world; building always takes more time and money than you ever think possible. We were still living amongst concrete brick and mounds of slack and sand, waiting for the builders to pick up where they had left off. Her youngest children loved playing in the sand and for a while they were bringing their sheets out to the sand mound every night and sleeping on it. In the mornings we took our sweet tea, peeping at each other between concrete pyramids.

The second thing that people in Kuajok always pointedly told me was, 'this place has been very well surveyed.' The grid is indeed precise and impressive. There are new inequalities between rich and poor but there is nothing so remarkable about that. What is different is that Kuajok's ordered grid is also under assault from temporal inequalities between the past and the future. This disparity is not only about prosperity and destitution, but how a place deals with its violent birth.

History has hung around here in some quirky ways. In South Sudan the biggest international presence is no longer the British Empire. Now it is the United Nations. But, the UN boss here is the son of the last British Commissioner. He lives in the guarded base of the edge of town. The Austrian missionary Nebel is long gone, but Egyptian nuns live in the missionaries' old houses. Formal Independence, with a new currency, new dialing code, government rebranding and all the trappings of sovereignty creates an illusion that there can be a break with the past, a new beginning. After all, it was quite literally the birth of a nation. But a complete break, however much longed for, is unobtainable. Amidst all the construction and renewal, the past is seeping back in.

Connections to North Sudan are still an everyday fact of life. Go to the market, and to the corner shops, and many of the traders you will find are from Darfur, stocking products from the North, although the amounts dwindled while I was there, gradually being replaced by goods from East Africa. For a while you could find 'Pasgianos', a luridly sweet fizzy drink, the flavor of children's cough mixture, the first soft drink to be bottled in Khartoum. The man with a shop near to our house had left a wife and two small children in South Darfur. We frequently struggled to communicate through a limited mutual comprehension of either Arabic or English. He made the journey by truck, illegally over the border. He says he is making money, he is sending it back to Nyala.

People, as well as products are still coming from the North. There is an area of Kuajok, known as Khartoum Jadid, 'New Khartoum'. Its where those who were displaced to North Sudan, during war, are now returning in their thousands. Many don't know Dinka and only speak Arabic. They have opened little shisha cafes and eat Northern-style food; little reminders of lives left behind as they adjust to a homeland many have never seen before. Some people were worried by this seeming separation, but as Kuajok expands, Khartoum Jadid, once little more than a camp on the outskirts, is blurring in with the rest of the town. Two ladies, who came from Abyei via Khartoum have the best restaurant in town; that is something everyone can agree on.

John Garang's Eden, the one he fought for, was something ancient. This Eden is a messy mix of the past and the future, still a work in progress. In the patch of Eden called Kuajok hundreds of trees have been felled and thousands of people have moved in, Adut is still building her house and the town is edging further out towards the swamp.

About the author:

Zoe Cormack is a PhD student at Durham University. Her thesis is about historical memory in Warrap State, South Sudan

MY ODE TO AZZA
by Lama El Hatow

My visit to Khartoum was a purely professional arrangement for a conference on the Nile Basin, that turned into the most personal and heartfelt encounter. I fell in love with a nation so rich in diversity, so humble in kindness, and so warm in its people. Myself, an environmental engineer, engrossed in the science and hydrology of this river that navigated 11 countries including my own, for the first time truly understood the spiritual and divine power these waters have over me.

At the confluence of the Blue and White Niles in Khartoum comes the convergence of cultures, ethnicities, and a truly romantic encounter. The Blue Nile brings its brownish colored waters from the Ethiopian highlands rich in sediment, nutrients and forcefulness. These rough waters as they materialize at the Gorge in Ethiopia slowly begin to calm in nature as they head towards Sudan. The White Nile brings its clear and pristine waters from Uganda, traveling across tropics and forests to reach Khartoum where its union with the Blue Nile is a destined and fated marriage. This union is often referred to as the longest kiss in history, as the two waters remain unmixed for kilometers. A breathtaking sight between two distinctly different colored waters flowing together in harmony and peace. These waters bring with them the stories and identities of the people along the Nile, and the harmony that is created in its simplicity. The diversity of our cultures along the Nile is rich and vibrant, and as we search for a space to hold a common ground for peace and stability across the Basin countries, we have forgotten the very essence of what these Nile waters hold. The confluence in Khartoum, an ever so beautiful reminder of this harmony, is a blissful awakening to me and I hope many others.

Overlooking the White Nile sitting in a forest of woodlands having breakfast on these river's banks, while a tea lady brings us Tea and Falafel, I discuss with a friend the current political climate in Sudan. Sudan is transforming itself from within. An oppressed conservative society on the outside is brewing with change from within its various spheres. The conversations that ensued during my visit, whether they pertained to arts, culture, politics, or environment stimulated my thoughts. Change is coming in Sudan. And it is coming very soon.

There is so much potential coming out of Sudan. I was so fortunate to be able to attend a Nas With Notepads open mic night for stand-up poetry in one of the local art centers. It was like giving me a magnifying glass to see right into the souls of Sudanese youth. Their hopes, their dreams, their desires for their country, and their urge and passion to make it a better place, sung out in words so eloquently beautiful and with such eagerness to share. As an outsider, I couldn't help but feel privileged to witness such unraveling of their souls to an audience so incredibly receptive for change. Starving for change. I feel as though they have entrusted their inner most secrets to me, and for that I am humbled.

To the beautiful Sudan, to Azza, coming from the root of "Izza" meaning might and power, may your soothing powers reign ever so dear over me and all that come to you. For I will cherish your ma'azza in my heart always.

About the author:

Lama El Hatow is an Environmental Engineer based in Cairo, Egypt. She is the Co-founder of an NGO/think tank called the Water Institute of the Nile (WIN) that aims to find win-win solutions amongst civil socity and communities across the Nile River Basin for sustainable water management.

WHAT IF?
By Maha El-Mustafa

It felt like a burning claw had latched itself to my forehead. I could hear voices, unclear and muffled in the background. What happened, where was Mama? Where was Moosa?

The voices grew clearer as my hazed state started to give way. "Who opened the gate? I told you to leave it closed! The children! Pick her up gently! Oh God! Oh God!" I recognised that voice instantly; it was the familiar voice of Adam, our housekeeper.

I felt large, familiar arms turn me on my back and lift me off the ground. I tried so hard to focus on the face in front of me but it seemed as though every time an image sharpened, it was instantly snatched from view like autumn leaves caught in the middle of a windstorm, and then there was darkness.

I woke up in my bed, with my purple and blue floral duvet wrapped tightly around me. I looked around and everything seemed perfectly normal and for a minute I thought perhaps that I had had a rather realistic dream that involved Moosa, and Adam and someone else that I couldn't quite remember, and just as I contemplated getting out of bed and looking for Moosa I felt a surge of pain throbbing from behind my temple. "Aaaagh" I let out a tortured wail and my mother came charging into the room, followed by my father. "Darling are you in pain, my poor little darling". My mother's calming voice worried me. "What happened Mama?". They explained to me that someone had left the garden gate open and Moosa and I had wandered outside to play in the street, though we had been repeatedly told not to, and in the excitement of our games I ran out onto the road in front of a rickshaw and had been hit. Apparently we had been in hospital for a few days and I would wake and sleep, but now my condition was stable.

My father did not breathe a word; he just stood behind my mother with a look I had never seen before. Was it anger? Guilt? Fear? Or all of them at once? Finally after what felt like an eternity of silence, he leant down and kissed my hand tenderly and a raspy whisper came out: "you are never to play with that boy again," and with that he stood up, grand and full of posture and marched out of my room.

My school years were basic. I was an above average student that worked hard and played little. This eventually earned me a scholarship for a bachelor degree in Civil Engineering at Imperial College, London, which continued on to a master's degree. When I completed my academic quest in the United Kingdom, I returned to my hometown of Khartoum to commence work in my father's company.

I can still remember the day I returned. It was late August and it had been raining the previous night. The streets were muddy and driving was problematic. I pulled up into our street and felt a surge of sadness, 6 years later and nothing has changed. As I stepped out of the car, I took in a deep breath and found myself lost in memories. The gate, that tree, our neighbours' guard who rarely left his seat. I looked over the gate into our garden and saw a man washing the tyres of my father's car. I couldn't recognise him, probably a new worker, I thought to myself. As I pushed open the gate, the man turned around startled. "Welcome home Nada".

My jaw dropped. "Moosa?" I couldn't believe my eyes. He was so grown; he was a man for God's sake. Well why wouldn't he grow up, I had. He walked over and hugged me hello and I felt something I hadn't felt since I left Sudan, warmth.

I heard someone clear their throat and I instantly pulled away, it was my father. I ran over and hugged him awkwardly and into the house we entered.

I never once stopped thinking about Moosa during my time in London, and I never quite understood why. I knew that we were the best of friends as children but that didn't explain why I found myself missing him and no one else, or why I wished he could visit London and I could show him all my favourite places. When I saw him the day I arrived I knew why. I loved him.

I always had it in my nature to feel quite ambivalent towards people. I struggled to understand a lot of the social norms that surrounded my circle. This made it harder for me to socialise, and most of the time I just wanted to be with Moosa. But the more time I spent with him, the more my father grew suspicious and agitated.

Moosa and I spoke a lot of marriage and life and dreams, and we always seemed to be on the same wavelength. Moosa used to say that we shared a soul and I believed him, he was my soul mate.

By the time I reached 25, I knew what I wanted in life, I wanted success, I wanted love, I wanted family, I wanted memories and I wanted to share all of that with Moosa.

Then one day, Moosa did the unspeakable, he approached my father and asked to speak to him about the possibility of marrying his daughter. The bewildered and almost insulted look on my father's face spoke volumes even amidst his silence. He simply put his hand on Moosa's shoulder and walked past him. Moosa was sad but not shocked.

My father knew that if he did not act quickly he would lose his daughter's reputation, and therefore his esteemed social position. With no discussion or consideration to me, I was wed to my cousin, a Doctor who studied in Ireland and was now working in Scotland.

Moosa himself eventually married a lady from his father's village and bore two sons from her. He eventually left our house and started working as a messenger in a German company. I haven't seen him since.

I have three children, I am a housewife, I am happy but not content, I am regretful but not bitter, I accept my fate, but I will forever wonder what if?

About the author:

I was born in the United Kingdom, where I have spent most of my life except for 8 wonderful years that were spent in Sudan. I love creativity, be it art, photography, writing or music. My biggest inspirations are the two main men in my life, my father and my husband.

HE CALLED IT AN INSECT
By Aziz El Nur

It had just been a normal day. It was mid-September, the rainy season was well advanced and the fields all looked lovely with the dense lush green sorghum plants. The ground outside in the camp area being damp, we had just put the food on the rattan mat on the ground inside one of the huts to have our lunch when two men we knew came walking in.

One was a young chap called Abdel Galeel, from the North of Sudan, and Bahar, a local younger boy. They worked for an organization called The Soil Maintenance Department, a kind of agricultural extension setup. They had absolutely no facilities to work with. Their tractor had broken down the day before and they had started walking to the nearest town to get a spare part. Anyway, when they reached us they were in complete shock. Abdel Galeel would not talk at all and refused to eat. Bahar was shocked too but had a couple of mouthfuls of food just to be polite. We then brought in the tea and managed to find out from Bahar that while walking the previous day, carrying their torches and walking sticks, it had become dark and they heard a sound in front of them. On switching on the torch they discovered a lion four meters away, standing looking at them. They all stood rooted in their spot.

"Then what happened?" I asked Bahar.

"The lion reacted", he said.

"What do you mean reacted?"

"He stood looking at us for what seemed like forever and then just turned round and walked away".

The incident had happened about 18 hours earlier. After lunch, I decided it best to drive them to El Damazin. Anyone who has worked or lived in the wilderness of Sudan knows just how easy it is to move on to "The Other Side".

When I moved to this area a few years earlier with a friend to try our luck farming, my friend had gone a few miles further into the bush to set up camp. One day he came round first thing in the morning and told me he had shared his hut with someone who had been roaming the area for a long number of years. Anyway, when they had finished chatting my friend had got up from his bed to turn off the lantern. His companion told him to leave the light on as it kept away the insects. My friend laughingly told him that it was a known fact that light attracted insects.

"Not these insects," said the visitor "these are large insects".

My friend on querying him found out that the he meant lions, leopards and a variety of other wild cats. He asked him if he had ever encountered any. He said sometimes but had only got into a scrap once, with a leopard. When my friend asked him who won his reply was "I'm still here aren't I?" The secret he said was to always carry a very large stick and to either have your back to a tree or someone who has his back to you. No way should you let him get to your back. He was also given a demonstration as to where to aim exactly when hitting the assailant.

My friend told me all this and then said he was going home. I said, "But you just got here".

"No" he said "I'm going Home home. Back to Omdurman".

"Why?" I asked.

Looking at me in amazement as if I had not comprehended anything, he said, "He called the lion an insect".

"A large insect" I said.

"Sure," said my friend "but an insect nonetheless, you stay and fan them away".

But I digress somewhat.

On getting to town in the evening and seeing the asphalt roads and street lights, things began to improve markedly in my companions' demeanour. They became a bit more relaxed with a less worrying look in their eyes. I dropped them off at their organisation's place of residence and went off to find my own sleeping arrangements.

The next afternoon I met Abdel Galeel and he was almost back to the normal person I had known previously. He told me that he had once visited the zoo in Khartoum and had had to leave never to return on seeing the lion. He told me that the only thing in life that he feared was the lion and for him to come up to him like that in the middle of nowhere was his worst nightmare come true. And, I kid you not, this was long before Adil Imam, but he said he never sat on the front row in the cinema for fear of the lion. He told me that was it. He was going north in a couple of days never to return. One minute you're right there…then something slips.

About the author:

Born in London (quite a while ago now). Come from Sudan. Live in London. Married. No pets. Four Children. Hate change, love routine. Have a simple life, but too complicated to be on Facebook. Would have loved to have retired back to Sudan, but as that is still looking impossible I'll take the Bahamas.

TEA LADY
by Islam Elamin

Walking towards the main street during my holiday, on a beautiful Friday afternoon, I begin to feel bombarded with all the bustle from those waiting to catch the bus or rickshaw (three wheeled vehicle).

Observing all the opening shops and the children waiting for the school bus anxiously, I find myself following the mist of the Bakhoor (Sudanese incense) taking me to a scene one can hardly miss, creating a relaxing atmosphere under a cool shadow of a tree along the Nile. There she is, sitting proudly at the centre of the circle of hope, surrounded by all her bottles of ingredients such as Ganzabel (ginger), Habaha (Cardamom), Nana (mint), Gerfa (cinnamon), cloves, tea, coffee and sugar followed by a unity of small shiny tea cups and shimmering tea spoons all forming her front façade, and to her side a Kanuun (handmade grill) filled with hot burning charcoal on top of which is placed a golden yellow pot, boiling with hot water, ready to be united with the rest of the ingredients. Another Kanuun sits with a frying pan roasting coffee beans; the smell pleasantly overwhelming as I approach. I see men stepping out of their cars into the gleaming sun, ordering and drinking their tea, rushing, bidding their quick goodbyes before leaving to work. I glance around as my eyes fall and see two couples gazing, with love, at each other, each one indulging in a bite of Legamat (Sudanese doughnut) followed by a sip of tea. Directly behind them are two students revising together with a cup of tea in one hand, and a book in the other. I look to my right and grasp a group of men proudly laughing, dressed in the traditional white Jalabiya (men's garment) and Ema (a head cover) and Markoob (men's shoe), all groomed as if heading towards another celebration. At that moment a soft sound leads my ears to a little group of friends harmonising. One hits the table making a beat, whilst the others naturally join in clapping and singing wistfully. Towards the centre a man sits stiffly looking worried as she comforts him. Minutes after her incoherent speech to him, he abruptly beams with a smile as his mood changes; her face is also painted with a big smile and with several reassuring nods she wipes off her sweat of exhaustion. She continues with a welcoming smile, her face so comforting.

I happily walk towards her and order my tea. She looks up at me, a smile immediately visible. "How are you my daughter?" she greets me. I feel at ease as if she was my long lost aunt. We start to converse. The gathering of people brings a different taste to my tea as I drink it.

I learn that her husband has passed away and financially her situation was not enough to support her family. She takes five photos out of her purse and tells me "These are my daughters," she shows me the beautiful girls one by one. "This is when they were about your age; one finished her studies and is married to one of the customers I served." I begin to wonder if they help her, as if reading my mind she continues telling me that she does not want them to come and help her as she thinks they might feel uncomfortable with some of the customers that don't always have the right intention, she adds that she wants them to focus on their studies. Zoning out into my thoughts I begin to see how she has managed to encourage so many people to start a small business just like her to make a living.

A cool breeze hits us as I watch her fan the heat of the charcoal inside the Kanuun with her Hababa (handmade Sudanese fan). I am flooded with information of Sudanese traditional ornaments such as: Sebha (used for worshipping), Wadey (used by Fortune tellers, Tabag (used to cover food and keep it warm), Mubkhar (used to hold charcoal which is sprinkled with incense) Henna (form of decoration for married woman), Ladaya (cooking pot), Doraya (a bowl used to carry liquids), Dahaloob (a bowl made from clay used to boil milk), Mufraka (wooden spoon), Saaj/Dooka (used to make traditional Sudanese food), Toub (traditional women's clothing), Rababa (handmade musical instrument), Nehas (used on occasions to make sound), Zeer (used to store cool water), Fundug and Madag (used to crush herbs), Gufa (used to carry groceries), Mashleeb (used to store the food far of reach of animals), Kantoosh (used to store milk), handmade jewellery (made from local materials), Zaaf (used to make bags, carpets, food, coverings, and house interior walls), Ebreg (container to store water for waduu), Sahara (a box used for storage) Lamba/Ratena (used as an alternative during power cut), Kabdolo (a container used to store milk), Kas (a cup used for drinking), Ferka (a decorative cloth used by the bride during her wedding entrance), Gerba (used to carry water to keep cool), Wesada (handmade pillow), Hijab (used for protection against evil), Seneyat Al-jirtik (used to carry perfume for the bride), Lohan (wooden board used with charcoal to write the Quranic verses during memorising the Holy Quran). Goteya (house made of clay), Rakooba (a canopy), Sareef (a fence), Sageya (manually generated to supply water from river to plants), Banbar (a chair), Angareb (homemade bed).

I learnt she is full of different stories from the people she has served, she really is a glimpse of hope; not only does she enjoy what she does but is also proud of raising her children, some of them now successful members of society. She comforts, welcomes and brings hope to those around her; she is part of the Sudanese culture. I have so much respect for her, who is she?

Sit Alshay (Sudanese tea lady).

She is one example of many tea ladies in Sudan. I learnt from her that no matter how hard life gets and the challenges that are thrown your way, there is always hope. She is a very simple lady that brings joy and happiness to those around her.

About the author:

My name is Islam Elamin. I used to live in Umdurman, Sudan but I am currently a university student living in London. I have volunteered to assist children at a Sudanese community school, working with children in nursery. I am also an active member of the Youth Factor, helping with planning and organizing academic and cultural events for the Sudanese community.

Illustration by Hussein Merghani

THE OLD WAYS
by Asiya Elgady

Sitting in the kitchen, squashed around a dining table too big for its space so that we three were packed in around the edges, confined between the walls, the cabinets and each other. It was here that I found myself caught in a photograph, a sepia-toned Polaroid, already worn around the edges, creased as delicately as laughter lines when it found me. Head down and far away from it all, I was so enraptured by mundane happenings that looking back I chuckle, knowing full well it was the calm before the storm. Except this storm was electrifying. No destruction and desolation lay waiting for me on the other side of this. Instead it tore through the galaxies of my thoughts with a voracious force, unapologetic and defiant. Like most natural forces it possessed a strength and sagacity that guided its course, so that it knew how to undo what had been done and with that the storm ripped through the fabric of my life. As the fibres unravelled, the thoughts that formed the strands of my knotted mind melted and slowly dissipated. But that calm, that calm, is what I seek to remember. For as lessons in life go, I wish to remember this one for those inevitable long and haunting nights to come. Never mistake the lull before the chorus for the end of the song.

Cloistered by the thoughts encompassed by this lull, entirely unaware of this moment I was in, I was there but in a parallel time where we three limbs of the same person existed in secluded fusion; them and me. And just like that I raised my head, such a small and innocuous act. With that slightest tilt, I noticed, the glow of the room, the warmth of the atmosphere, and suddenly I was immersed. Flung so far and so fast across those parallel planes, the momentum both catapulting and cradling me, I felt hurled into a rare moment of lucidity. Everything was brighter, clearer, more vivid, and what's more I could see the light in her eyes, caused by her smile, dancing playfully; inflecting and refracting, ebbing and flowing in the subtlety of her nods and the movement of her hands.

It was in this moment, the air heavy with sweet smells borne of memories long since buried, that I saw my mother; a vision I had not seen for a little more than a while. Some eight years of a while. Not a spectre, nor a waking dream, but a re-imagining in a different form. There she was, in the light, in that smile. It was her. Mama.

This transcendent moment was shrouded in a crystallised heart; itself full and glowing for lack of chips or scratches. Iridescent. Forever suspended in a chasm of fallowed potential. Never to be realised but in the ethereal dreams crafted by a mind striving tirelessly, desperately, to protect and shroud itself from the harshness of truths too painful to bear. Weaving a rich tapestry of ornate paracosms, each thread delicately working the shattering pain into a million little specks to be unravelled in their own time. Yet here I was, suspended like the crystallised heart, coming undone in the electric storm, all within this one moment.

It was then that I realised, looking between these two women, an expanse of years separating their words and actions, from me, that there was something beautiful about the old ways. Something untouched by the cold of this weather, nor the harshness of this time. And in those old ways, I found something. Something indescribable, innate and encompassing, but nonetheless something tacit. Something of myself. It was Sudan.

As this moment fell gracefully and tenderly into place it nestled comfortably, in that space in my chest, between my lungs and ribs. And all at once I watched the familiar ache, I then knew to be longing, dull until it flowed out and away; soothed by this moment. All the while enveloped by its warmth, its glow. Delicately fitting and filling deep into the roots once ingrained with gaping, longing, nothingness, and now transfused with incandescent splendour.

I had been broken, I had been shattered and I had been dispersed to the farthest regions of an abyss. And much like this crystal heart, it was beautiful. A million specks of light spread across an entire span of a potential life woven into a paracosm, a sanctuary, and it was beautiful. "A foul and awesome display". Yet the re-placing, the finding and the fixing, felt right. It felt good. It, finally, felt whole. It is okay to be broken. It is okay to be fixed. And with that I began fixing.

This tacit something, vindicated by experience and remnant of being broken and scattered, was the first solitary piece to be returned to its rightful place; in me. So let it pass into my children and take its rightful place in them. Let them know my Sudan. Let them find themselves, as I did. Let them love themselves, as I have. Let them learn, as I learnt. That for all the distance of land, between three people, nothing quite isolates and polarises like the distance of age. It permeates everything, exacerbates everything, leaving nothing, no thought or feeling, untouched.

So I learnt, and I continue to learn, that no matter where I was or whom I'd lost, no matter the circumstances, it would have been hard. It would have been painful. It would have broken and destroyed me. And I would have survived.

Making the fruits that I reap, borne of a Sudanese mango tree whose roots now flowed with crystallised speckles, as sweet as the fruits I once shared with her. My mother. My mama.

This. This moment, like so many others I have known, was one of those special ones; to keep and treasure, to guard, and hold close. A crystal heart, to rarely show another soul. So often in the longing, I feared that she had given me nothing, and that without her I would be nothing. But in that moment I saw, this is what she gave me. My strength. My smile. My Sudan.

About the author:

Being in the purgatory of a law conversion, I really enjoy the different aspects of creative writing, as they connect me to Sudan's rich cultural and linguistic heritage. I also love singing, cooking (eating) and travelling. Yeah - for want of a proper sit-down, this clichéd image is actually quite accurate.

WAHID SUDAN
by Dikun Peace Elioba

"Sudan is not really a country at all, but many. A composite of layers, like a genetic fingerprint of memories that were once fluid, but have since crystallized out from the crucible of possibility".

Jamal Mahjoub

The silhouette of Sudan
used to look beautiful
as it pierced from the Nubian roots of civilization
triumphed by a vast land.
Surpassing all other countries in Africa in size
my mother used to take pride in Sudan
since I was young.

I cannot help but gaze at its shape now
As my mind becomes enraptured in ambivalence
and my eyes shift in awe and despise
because it's so easy to focus on the dividing line
instead of what lies omnipresent within and through:
Wahid Sudan bes!

Wahid Sudan may only thrive
from its interconnectedness
departed yet, attached
the same difference
We remain Sudanese
Wahid Sudan.

Almost as if we were never separated,
I meet you.
We connect in an instant
Even though politics will make us different
You say, "I love you"
We cherish our hidden knowledge
Because what we love about each other
Lies within the depth of our hearts
And not about borders.
You say, "We don't care about this separation".
We unite within the memories of a country that was there once
And still lingers internally,
Despite what it has now *become.*

Almost as if we were never separated,
We meet as one.
Amidst a conversation you utter
in a slow stirring tongue of confidence:
"Whenever someone asks me where I am from in Sudan
I never say North or South Sudan
I say I am from THE SUDAN
We are just going through a dark period."

Our cultures are still here
scattered in abundance.
Tribes remain the same tribes
And languages are still spoken in its mother tongue.
Even Sudanese Arabic is varied
spoken differently depending on our location.
We have even moulded our language
to fit our local and most intimate heritage.

Just as a circle
holds within its structure parts
These partitions form its existence as a whole.
We were always one
like a puzzle piece
Assorted by natural differences
But through our differences we were always still pieces
Of what made us *Sudanese*.

There is in fact a Wahid Sudan.
It is the truth of history that we go back to
It is the truth within our history that we go back to
In order to understand ourselves now.
It is beyond the reality of divisions
It is the living longing for a "New Sudan" everywhere.
Because even though it may not be physically present
It lives within the realms of dreams and yearning
to be created into a future reality.

And if it may not be tangible in the future
It did exist somewhere
Bilad as Sudan
Wahid Sudan is the Old Sudan.

There is a border that divides us
but if one looks closely
and closes their eyes
what is the truth in memory?
And what is the difference that remains?

It is merely the politics and creation of a line!
Wahid Sudan bes!

About the author:

Dikun is an undergraduate student majoring in International Relations and Cultural Studies. She lives in New York and is South Sudanese. She is interested in Sudanese and South Sudanese politics and aspires to express her passion for the Sudan's through her personal creative writing and international and global studies.

THE BLACKOUT
by Yasir Elkhidir

I went to Sudan a couple of weeks ago. As soon as I reached my sweet home, I greeted everyone and had a laugh with my family members, who were very glad to meet me after two years of staying abroad. I was very tired from traveling, my trip exceeded 30 hours and I was so grateful to finally reach home. I ate some food and went to have a shower before going to bed. I entered the shower, hung my clothes on the wall, held the soap in one hand and turned the tap for the shower with the other hand. I closed my eyes and prepared myself emotionally and psychologically for the first drops of cold water to start hitting my head and my shoulders. I even remember shivering in advance. After 10 seconds of absolute fear, nothing happened, so I opened my eyes slowly and gave the tap another turn then quickly closed my eyes and waited for a few more seconds. When nothing happened again I opened my eyes, opened the shower door slightly and shouted loudly, "Hey, what's wrong with the water?"

A reply came from far away. "Water? Oh, they didn't tell you? It's been out since the morning!" At that moment and after hearing this, I was seriously considering packing my stuff and going back to the airport, but then I remembered that I have been in worse conditions.

At that dry moment of my life and while I was wearing my dirty clothes again, I had some flashbacks. I remembered back in the days when I was studying in my college in Sudan, the days of "Blackouts" as I used to call them. When the electricity was so bad it would sometimes go out on a daily basis and stay out for several hours. I used to discover this electricity shortage only after I reached home from a long tedious day. The electricity itself was not the issue; the electricity was just the cherry on the cake.

The 'cake' was my daily routine, which was somehow totally different to the routine of those students we see laughing and studying in movies and university advertisements. I used to wake up late every single day, sometimes I would be in such a rush that I would have to put my shoes on while going to the toilet. I did not have a mirror at all so I had to wash my face, comb my hair and brush my teeth blindly. In fact, most of the time, I skipped the hair part and I can still recall putting my toothbrush in my pocket a couple of times and finishing this business when I reached the college.

The next step was to run like a thief to save a few minutes. Run from my house to the main road where public transportation was available. This also terminated whatever cleanliness and tidiness I had (if any), because it's not exactly like I was running in the green grass hills of Switzerland, it was all sand and holes. While running towards the road, there are usually three situations every person faces. Situation number one is when the bus arrives before you reach the main street and it's loaded with passengers or almost loaded. When that extra guy (me) is running far away, waving and screaming to stop the bus but it's not really worth it. The bus will only slow down far away (not stop) and you have to increase your running speed to catch anything to pull you up in this moving vehicle. You can grab the door, the door handle, the side of the window, the bus conductor (komsari) and/or the shirt of any passenger standing on the steps of the door. The most important thing is to stay alive by keeping at least one, or part of one foot inside the bus in order not to fall and break your neck. Situation number two is when the bus is not that full, and it comes just seconds before you arrive and stops for you. It gives you the feeling that it stopped just for you, but actually when you get on and sit down you find the conductor still outside waving to people so far you can barely see them, so you have to wait for another few minutes, but at least you get a seat. On some occasions you face situation number three, which is the no-bus situation. This situation is not as bad as the others because after 15 or 20 minutes of delay you lose hope of catching the lecture on time, and you get to have some "quality" time to sit and drink some good Sudanese coffee (Jabana) with the tea lady in the local market, which was midway between my home and the college.

Riding public transportation is another story in itself. The nice thing about public transportation is that it is really public. All types of society and different types of people take public buses in Sudan. You can find yourself cramped between a doctor and an engineer talking about politics or economy on one side, and between another laborer and a lemon juice stand keeper arguing about the same topic on the other side. No one, and I repeat no one, in Sudan doesn't know anything about everything! I have never heard the word "I don't know" from the Sudanese nation of public transportation. Whether it's right or wrong, everyone is throwing in their own theories and opinions (as facts) in history, geography, sociology, politics and even medicine. Even the bus conductors, who are usually busy collecting the extra 100 (equivalent to 10 pence), from the usual 40 year old guy pretending to be a student, sometimes join the public talk.

When the bus reaches the first destination, which is the local market, I check the time. If I have already missed the lecture, I am too late or I want to save myself the embarrassment of being rejected by the lecturer at the door of the class, I go to have the quality time with the tea lady. If not, the running procedure starts again from the bus to one of the community taxis (al-taxi al-ta'awni) which are extremely old mini buses assigned to work in the rural areas of Khartoum. They have no door handles of course, so to get in you have to reach your hand inside through the place where there was a window 30 years ago. Then you pull the high-tech rope that is somehow tied to the door handle inside the car body. You enter to find the floor filled with big see-through holes that lead to outside and can fit a wallet or a phone, so any dropped belongings might end up directly on the street. The seats, especially the folded ones on the side, are almost always back-breakingly tilted. The noise and the vibration give you the feeling that you are a banana inside a kitchen blender. The smell terminates whatever was left of your cleanliness. After reaching the final stop, either you walk your way through more sandy dirt, or settle for a one Sudanese pound, noisy, three-wheeled vehicle (Raksha) to reach the college.

Reaching the college is an achievement in itself. Life gets slightly easier after that, with normal lectures and seminars like any other decent student in the world. The Sudanese-ness starts again at lunch time in the local cafeteria. One of my daily routines was to fight with the staff there. I am not an aggressive person at all and I am very peaceful in general, but, in my opinion, it is extremely unacceptable and weird to fill the meat sandwich (shawerma) with carrots and green pepper and even stranger to put fried eggs and a whole olive, with its stone, in a burger. You start enjoying your burger when suddenly you hear a painful crack, and you spit out to find a stone and a small piece of your tooth! Who created this recipe!

Going back from the college was similar to the trip in the morning but in a backward manner. The only differences were that there was less rush, less energy, more exhaustion and an excessive amount of sun and heat. I survived though.

Now imagine how it was, for someone like me, coming back from college after going through all of these things. The ultimate dream of such a person is to have a good shower, turn on the air conditioner and have a nap. Here is where the Blackout stood out from the crowd and represented that cherry on top of the cake. Imagine reaching home and finding out that the electricity is out and you have to sleep in the heat. Imagine waking up with the electricity still out and having to light a candle to study. Candles are not that romantic when they start gathering mosquitoes around their light. The only advantage of this is when I will have kids later; I can say, "When I was your age, I used to study by candlelight". It wasn't fun back then, but it's definitely a cool thing to say. In fact my whole memory of Sudan, regardless of the difficulties I had, was enjoyable and they were truly the best days of my life. I guess a little struggle adds spice to anyone's life.

About the author:

I am Yasir Elkhider, a 30-year-old Sudanese dentist, who is engaged. I am currently studying and living in China. I started writing 10 years ago under "kalam sai" which is now a Wordpress blog. I write in both Arabic and English, and have a column in 500 words magazine "Random rants" section; every now and then I write a political piece in the Rakoba online newspaper. The one common factor in all of my articles: ALL are sarcastic and nothing is serious, I like laughter!

KHARTOUM, SUDAN 1988-1991
by John D. Ewart

We arrived in late April 1988: one British Council officer, one wife and one 1-year old, plus 6 overweight suitcases and at least 40 kilos of baby cereals, baby powders, baby lotions and diapers. All purchased in those superbly stocked supermarkets in Dubai (our previous posting) and mostly from Spinneys, an institution which had figured prominently in Kitchener's march southwards in 1898.

A three-hour flight from Dubai, and as we neared our destination we felt the excitement of seeing the Nile for the first time: that mighty waterway that had inspired the imagination of Herodotus and that elusive vision of the "Mountains of the Moon"; the heroics of Sir Samuel and Lady Baker; the derring-do of Burton, Speke (and Speke's tragic end) and Livingstone; the thrilling prose of Churchill's "The River War" and Alan Moorhead's cascade of events and characters - General Gordon, Kitchener, the "Mahdi" et al.- in "The White Nile" – but where is that river? It's not that dismal brown stream down below, is it? We could see the loop north of the capital that gave Khartoum its name – but the river was a mere trickle of grubby water. "Ah," we said to ourselves, "maybe when it rains." Just a few months later – on a Thursday evening in early August to be precise – the river responded.

So, from the comforts of Dubai to dusty, crowded Khartoum to be greeted on the 15th May with the Acropole Hotel bombing followed by the tragic death (in a car accident) of our senior ODA advisor. Then our first 'haboob' – what next?

But, first of all, the paperwork: forms completed, a mountain of photographs and off to the Ministry of the Interior where I waited – and waited – and was eventually asked to come back at a later and unspecified date. The waiting continued for three weeks: I decided that enough was enough and that I would sort this out myself.

A genial Colonel greeted me: "We apologise, Mr. John, but there are formalities". I replied that I wanted to get on with my work, and had to travel outside the capital to see our projects and meet the teaching staff, so I needed the appropriate clearance and travel document. "Our work is in education and scholarships. I'm not a spy or a terrorist." said I.

More apologies – "We understand, Mr. John, but we must be careful: the problem is that you have a beard and you speak Arabic – pause - and, - pause - you understand, don't you? Eventually the 'i-qAma' was provided and I was free to travel.

A smile, a handshake and a parting shot from the Colonel with an unforgettable twinkle in his eye – "You need not worry – I know your office: many years ago I was a British Council scholar".

Work began, and I went out of Khartoum to Umdurman, to al-Obayd, to Wad Madani, where we had a teacher training project at the University, and then an unofficial detour and a sneak into the past with a visit to Atbara railway station: so many relics of Sudan Railways – magnificent 4-6-0's (Swindon built?) all gathering dust and looking so forlorn, rather like unsold toys on the shelves at Christmas time as if saying "Won't somebody come and drive me? I used to be so strong and shiny – and I could whistle, too."

Then back to Khartoum and to its institutions - SELTI, ISETI and the University. I met many of the Sudanese academics who spoke such fluent and idiomatic English: my grammatically correct but rather clumsy Arabic paled in comparison.

I remember well going to the office of one of the senior officials in the University. My visit followed "an incident' in the university grounds and the Police were involved - and so few of the 'incidents' related to academic matters. I asked the official how he was feeling.

The reply: "Mr.John, I am well. I think you would say "tikkatiboo" – would you not?" These highly educated and articulate academics had all read their Shakespeare, their Milton, Dickens – and Kipling.

So, to early August: seven forty-five one Thursday evening - off into the town centre to get some milk for our son. I parked outside the grocer's shop (a quick call so I left the engine running) walked in, exchanged a few greetings, bought the milk and commented on the sound of the rain which had just started, and went outside. A matter of ten minutes in the shop and I could only see half the front wheel of the Landrover – it was bucketing down: the rain spurting up from the road had stopped the engine but with a helpful push from a few sturdy passers-by I got off again and drove home almost blindly with the windscreen wipers doing their best to fight off the rain but failing.

Arrived home, raced in (soaked) with aforementioned milk and listened to the thunderous noise of the rain pounding on the roof. Suddenly it was 8.30 - then 9 and then 9.30 - ten o'clock came and 11 and 12 - and the rain drummed on. This was frightening: no ordinary downpour. When was it going to stop? (I don't like water – can't swim, in fact, as a result of an unfortunate accident in Scotland, but that's another tale).

And then we noticed a little trickle of water slithering into the house underneath one of the front doors – like a Wyndham triffid – and we had seven doors, two at the front, three at the back and two to the side: we raced round the house and, sure enough, the water was coming in under all seven doors.

Unfortunately the house was below the level of the tarmac road beyond the garden - which was now flooded and glistened beneath the moon – and there was nothing to stop the water. A quick check on our son – sleeping upstairs and blissfully oblivious of the little drama downstairs; but, looking at the living room floor, our next thoughts were how to save that priceless, much-travelled Morocccan carpet (so many memories of that coveted treasure - the prize after four hours of hard bargaining and litres of coffee in the souq in Fes, Morocco)

Carpet rolled up and upstairs to safety: meanwhile the drumming outside continued and the water in the house rose (eventually, after eight hours, to 18 inches). Next to be saved were the gramophone records (some bought in the 1950's when my mother and I saved our threepenny pieces to pay one pound, seventeen shillings and sixpence for a gem from HMV, Decca records, Deutsche Grammophon and so on). This to be followed by more staggering upstairs – and our 1-year old slept on – perhaps dreaming of sunny days and croquet on the lawn?

Next shelf up were the books all getting nearer to a watery grave: but we did not intend to lose our first editions of Wilfred Thesiger's "Arabian Sands" or "The Marsh Arabs" (and complete with author's signature). Thesiger had served in Sudan during WWII. As the water rose we began to feel as Noah might have felt so long ago. Except that he had company.

At 4 am the rain stopped: we made a cup of tea, thanked our lucky stars and surveyed our ornament-free living and dining rooms – and then as the day dawned and the sun began to shine so the waters receded leaving nothing but brown streaks on the walls and the furniture. When an official came from our HQ in London his comment was "Yes, of course we've read about it in the papers but what floods are you talking about? Where?" The traces of 8 solid hours of rain disappeared in a matter of days.

First light Friday morning: a trip to the office which was five minutes' walk from the house – all well. It was situated just above the level of the roadway and thus safe from the rain. Then to our office and library in Umdurman – only a little water had entered the building but we had to cross the river – and then we saw why the 'mighty Nile' was so named: the trickle was no more – now a massive, half-mile wide expanse of swirling water breaking over its banks (hence all the water in Khartoum) and descending all the way from its source high in the Ethiopian mountains; millions of gallons of water on its way to the north sweeping much of Khartoum with it.

Saturday – the working week began: a devastated Khartoum. The floods had destroyed so much, and swept away buildings, fences, cars, pick-ups etc – and I waited for the Sudanese staff to arrive wondering what tales they would bring – and some of them had to travel several miles to get to the office.

But they arrived – some having walked for perhaps three hours and having lost land, fencing, animals, chickens, a kitchen wall, an outhouse: but when they reached the office there was no whining or complaining – the first question was "How are your wife and your son? Are they safe and well?"

We stayed in Sudan for three years; we did lots of things; we met lots of people and had lots of fun: but the most abiding, and cherished, memory is that moment of Sudanese loyalty and humanity.

A few years ago Edward, our elder son, (who slept through the flood) attended a wedding in Khartoum: a friend of his from schooldays in the UAE – and now a doctor – invited him to the ceremony and Edward enjoyed the best of Sudanese hospitality. He, too, has an abiding memory of a warm, welcoming and resolute people.

About the author:

John worked for the British Council for 30 years in Arab countries including Sudan (1988-1991). He and his wife, Inocenta, studied Arabic in Lebanon. From Yemen (YAR) and Algeria they moved to UAE where they have lived and worked for 20 years. They have two sons, both Arabic speakers.

MEMOIRS OF POSSIBILITY
by Shahd Fadlalmoula

Dear diary,

The air smelled heavy with tea, musk, and hope.

I followed the echoes of laughter as they led me to the patio. The sun was shying away from the horizon, and the clouds responded by cracking themselves open to reveal some pink and orange streaks of light that clashed with the clouds' bluewhite demeanor. It was almost magical, I thought. The sunsets never color the sky like this anywhere else.

I sat down, across from strangers. I mean, they were practically family, but I had only been around them for a few weeks. They spoke in hurried sentences, and blurs of hand motions. Sometimes, I tried to reach out and grab a word or two from under their lips, so I could decipher them later. But, whenever I pulled the words out of my pockets at night, they came out withered and empty. It's almost like they're wired to the souls of these people.

Such a shame, I would have loved to take some of their language away with me, when it was time to leave.

They didn't notice me, of course. These humans never do, but I sat there anyway. Looking for something out of the ordinary to capture with my pen. There was the mother I had been following around. She was wrapped in her usual array of colors streamed onto a long cloth they call thobe, which complemented the bundle of stories she carried under her half smile. Her long fingers, crinkled and soft, were wrapped around a white teacup that marked the coming of the afternoon in all the houses of this country. I don't know what the milky brown liquid in it tastes like, but to me it smells a lot like ritual. Which is comforting. I have always liked ritual, she is a loyal friend.

Then there were the others. They were quite odd puzzle pieces, but then again, this country is full to its brim with extraordinary pictures. This house had a little girl who wore her hair in two braids. Her name was Mona, and she was fresh with enthusiasm. I figure she's quite young, you know, because it shines brightest around her. But then again, you can never trust enthusiasm to tell you anything about age. These humans are unpredictable. Most of them dim down their enthusiasm as they grow older, but in my lifetime I've seen quite the number of outliers, I can tell you that! Anyways, Mona was sitting by the young man. I don't know what his name is, but they call him Jidu. I know that is code for grandfather in their language, but he had no withered skin, nor did wisdom come to visit him as often as it does all the other grandfathers I've seen. How strange.

Across from Jidu, on the other bed that took up half the length of the patio, sat the father. He sipped his tea while he flipped through pages of the world. I think they call it a jareeda. I suppose I've told you about it before, it's that fold of pages with pictures and words on it. The humans like to read it in the morning so that they can, later, talk about the things that happen on the other sides of the sea. Many of them put a lot of faith in it and believe what it tells them with very little reluctance, but not this father. He wears skepticism under his seeing windows. I've grown to like him, he's clever, I just wish he would lift this heavy veil he places between him and myself. He would be interested to learn of my adventures abroad. I could teach him a few things about change.

There was a knock on the door, and Jidu went to open it. Hails and greetings filled the air as a few of the father's friends walked onto the patio. The mother rose and walked into the house to bring some more white teacups from the kitchen. The knocks on the doors surprise me as an odd gesture, because no one really leaves their door closed around this time of the day. Everyone is expecting a visit at any time, although they never really know it's coming. It remains a mystery to me, but then again, many things about this country do.

The afternoon dragged on, and I was asked to leave the father and his friends' gathering because politics was coming. Politics wasn't a bad guy you know, but our chemistry usually doesn't allow us to coexist, at least not here. That's just how it is. So I followed Jidu around for a change. He was standing under a tree, whispering into a little box.

"I'm alright Alhamdulillah[2] , I just miss you. Yeah he's here, but I don't think they'll discuss any of the formalities today. My father is reluctant, but I told him it was secure enough... but... I know, but... I'm looking for one in Qatar, or the UAE... I don't know if I want to tear you away from... It isn't easy you know... You're all the family I want, but every home needs some ornaments too."

He sighed, and then began to talk about his day. His laughter was broken whenever it escaped his lips. I wondered who he was speaking to, although I figured it was a girl because these phone calls always made him wear that face. It was hard to describe what it looked like, but whenever I saw a boy wear it his heart declared its existence more loudly, and his nerves intertwined into butterflies and fell into his stomach. It was interesting to watch.

Anyway, that's almost everything noteworthy I remember about that day. The musk wore off, the tea was sipped dry, but hope lingered in the air. Something was coming.

⎯⎯◦◦◦⎯⎯

Dear diary,

I lurked around for a few months, and the time flowed about with grace. I was growing stronger, but I had an odd sense of isolation. I failed to understand it, never had I felt so alive, yet so invisible. This country was growing on me in uncanny ways.

The family was getting ready to celebrate Jidu's wedding. My friend joy was everywhere, fat and suffocating. Two days ago there was a full set of humans who came to

---

2   *Thank God*

the large red tent that was now standing in front of the house. The people here always built tents in front of their houses when they wanted to declare their occasions to the country. I think the tents are too small, because when these people come together to celebrate or mourn their loved ones, their joy or sorrow always manages to spill into the streets. I have never seen compassion shared like this before.

Gladly, this time around it was all joy. Jidu was getting married to the girl I was telling you about, the one that made him wear that face. I went to visit her once. I mean, I know I was assigned to this family, but I just had to see for myself who they were writing into their tree of kin. She lived right next door, and boy was she beautiful! Her eyes took up a glorified place over her cheeks, and they were deeper than any book I had ever read. There was a lot of enthusiasm glowing from her, and charm never left her side. Her hair danced about her waist, and reflected darkness the color of earth. She made her own music, which sounded like laughter, but better. Then there was her skin. It was a shade unique to this country, like the clash of two cultures was written into her cells. She looked like she hadn't been out of the house for a while. When I came to visit, she was sitting on a low stool with a large cloak wrapped around her. Smoke evaded her body wherever there was room between her and the cloak. It must have been some local sauna ritual. When she was done, her skin smelled like musk, and she was radiating from all the herbal delicacies that had left their marks on her skin. Anyway, I didn't stay with her for too long, someone else was assigned to her house. Thank god! I feared she would make me wear that face too.

The week was filled with music. On the first day people who looked like extended pieces of the family came to the red tent. They sat around Jidu and painted their hands black with soil. They called it henna. Jidu wore it around his hands and feet too. There was a woman with a drum who sang for them, her voice reminded me of my friend history. I would have to ask him about her someday. Anyways, it was one party after another. Often, the bride's family was invited and other times it was just my family's friends. The air always felt thick with community. Sometimes it became hard to tell who was a guest and who wasn't, everyone made themselves at home. Literally! I once saw a woman come from the house at the end of the block carrying a bucket of flour. She just marched into the kitchen and asked the mother to go to her room and rest. She then pulled a low stool and sat across a little firebox with a round, flat pan on it, and began to make a very thin, breadlike pastry. There were tens of women doing that, humming with joy as they exchanged stories about their own wedding days.

<hr />

Dear diary,

Today Jidu walked into a hall wearing the moon on his forehead. It was golden, crescentshaped, and wrapped around his head with a strap of red silk. He wore a white jalabeya[3] , the color of his immense happiness. It had streaks of red and gold, here and there. They say red is the color of new beginnings, I think that's why they're covered in it. As for the bride, she was wrapped in red, and her head was covered with gold. So were

---

3   *Anklelength white gown worn by men in the MiddleEast and Northern Africa*

her arms, which looked like canvases with deeply intricate henna paintings on them. The paintings matched the ones that stemmed from the souls of her feet to her knees. The couple was quite a sight for sore eyes.

The night dragged on. I danced about in the background. The music felt warm on my skin, its words leaking with meanings of tradition, and a long history of endurance that surfaced just beneath each beat of the drum. Some of them could see me, I know Jidu did. It must have confused him, since he had never sent out an invitation card with my name on it.

———◦◦◦◦◦———

Dear diary,

I feel awfully sick, I don't know why. The atmosphere is fogged with tension at the house these days. I keep getting messages from my boss telling me I'll have to leave soon, but I don't want to. If hope gets to stay, I think I should too!

Jidu and his bride left on their honeymoon to Dubai, and I was encouraged to go with them but I really didn't want to go on a vacation, to be quite honest. I have work to do here, I want to be seen again the way I was on Jidu's wedding night.

Just then, the little box rang. The father pressed a button and began talking into it. As usual, I had to keep my distance from him and the veil he kept between us, so I couldn't hear what he was saying, but he eluded an air of mixed emotions. He was happy, but it was the happiness a soldier carried on his back at the end of a long war. It came at the price of loss, and held lots of reluctant despair under its breath. That's when the mother came in, she took the box and talked into it, then she started crying.

"But we didn't even get to properly say goodbye... I understand ya walady[4] , just take care of your wife and don't forget about us. Bring me home some grandchildren, ok?"

She said her goodbyes and gave the box back to the father, as she sluggishly went to sit by him. He raised an arm and gently placed his hands on her shoulder, rubbing the sorrow out of her. She shook with worry, and wept. What was going on? What did Jidu do?

I coughed till I was unconscious, which didn't really matter. I was still very invisible, but now I barely felt alive.

———◦◦◦◦◦———

Dear diary,

The air smelled heavy with tea, musk and loss.

The last time I had seen Jidu, we spoke. I told you he had seen me, but when I formally introduced myself he responded in the most unexpected way you could imagine.

.
_____

4   *My son*

68

He laughed.

"This is impossible, you're supposed to be... umm..."

"Abstract?" I replied. "Yes, pretty much. Well, we are when we want to be."

"We?" he looked at me with confusion.

"Yeah, there are many of us. We come in different shapes and sizes. We're assigned to families, or individuals based on the cards life has dealt them. Anyway, I'm glad you can see me. There's a lot to be done in this country now that we've been formally acquainted."

"Don't you know? My wife and I are traveling out of the country tonight. We're going to Dubai."

"How lovely! I was in Dubai some years ago, I helped build that country, you know. Many others too. But I'll tell you about that when you're back. When will that be, by the way?"

"I don't know..." he had replied

Of course I didn't understand that he meant he had bought a one-way ticket. I didn't understand why he wanted me to come with him, or why he told me not to wait when I politely declined. I was an expert on waiting, I had told him. He only laughed.

Later, I found out that he had found a job there. I wish I had known, I would have told him to stay right here, in Sudan. He could have done so much more here, I could have helped him. But now that he has left, I'm forced to leave too. Otherwise I'll be bedridden till I no longer exist.

Maybe I will visit him in Dubai, and convince him to come back.

I wonder if someday Mona will to be ready see me; or if I'll be reassigned to this place I've grown to call home. I think about it all the time.

This place has grown on me in uncanny ways, I wish it was as welcoming as I know it could be. I wish I could stay longer, I could teach this land a few things about change.

With love,

Possibility.

About the author:

I am a young student who has been passionate about writing ever since I put pen to paper at the age of nine. I aspire to reintroduce my beloved country to the world, through my humble collection of stories and poems. I'm also a proud ice cream enthusiast, and a certified bookworm.

THE LIGHT IN THE DESERT
by Reem Gaafar
(HONOURABLE MENTION)

They came from the far north, a caravan of camels and donkeys and children, travelling through the desert and following the twists and turns of the Nile for months, until they found the place they and their children and grandchildren would call home: Al Barkal. Arab nomads that they were, the word home was always relative rather than absolute. They would settle down in the midst of other tribes, taking on their accents and adopting their clothing and lifestyles, but would always hold on to their own religious practices and poetry, keep their daughters and women indoors, marry only their cousins and socialize at a bare minimum. Some saw themselves as superior to their indigenous neighbours, while others just preferred to keep to themselves. Some cared only for their own and their families' wellbeing. While others were born with the compassion and foresight to see that their own and their families' wellbeing actually lay in the wellbeing of those around them.

The Gaafar Mustafa clan were successful merchants. Although not from the area they gradually took over the market, competing with the local merchants and expanding their businesses. They imported canned goods, perfume, material and shoes from Egypt, India and Holland. Their date gardens flourished in the hot and dry weather of the Northern state. They were generous with their money; a valuable secret to prosperity. Travelers would tell of times that they were lost in the desert without food or water, and would spot the distant lights of the Gaafar residence in the gloom, where they would be welcomed, fed and sheltered at a time where most people in the region didn't have so much to give away and so were not so free with their hospitality. During the date harvesting season, the less fortunate and still nomadic Arabs would gather on the dunes around the villages, their presence announced by their lighted fires at night with no roof over their heads but the sky. Again, not everyone gave away so freely, but dates both fresh and dried and lengths of damoriya to shelter from the cold were regularly dispatched from the Gaafar household. Also, at a time where slavery was still practiced openly and English and Sudanese head hunters would chase women and children into the caves of the Nuba mountains, throwing after them sacks of chilli peppers lit on fire to drive them out and noose them, there was not, ever, a single slave in any one of the Gaafar homes; a fact that they boasted about freely.

Mahgoub Gaafar was small for his age. When he started school his classmates would lift him up and plop him into the small falooka they would take across the Nile from the Karima side to Marawi, after which would start the long trek to Marawi Basic School. Back in the 1920s, an elementary education was the equivalent of a college degree in those sleepy villages of the Northern State, and an elementary education was what he got, after which he graduated into the world of trade and marketing. He came from a line of accomplishers, and had big boots to fill. His father, Gaafar Mustafa, was already a wealthy merchant by then, who boasted several shops and palm tree gardens, and whose house on top of Jabal Om Hamad had front gates large enough to admit a full-grown camel carrying huge sacks of dates on its back to deposit in the front yard. His grandfather,

Mustafa Mohamed, had been the one to guide the English railway from Shandi down to Kareema, as he and his older son Mahgoub led the tracking team through the desert that only nomads can negotiate with the help of the stars and the direction of the wind. They and their cousins were also in charge of delivering the national mail across the country; the first postal stamp of Sudan is adorned with one of their sons' picture. And their forefathers before them had an equally impressive job as it was at their time: they were Hambata, a glorified version of highway men who refused to succumb to the occupation, and who cut off and looted Turkish tax-collectors carrying Sudanese tax money north.

Mahgoub Gaafar fell naturally into the family business, and started off with a small shop given to him by his father, which was closed in punishment and opened the next day whenever he would do something wrong. With time, his own business grew, as his sweet demeanor and cheerful and friendly manner made him popular amongst the villagers. The richer he became, the more modest he proved himself to be; he would pray on an old sack in front of the shop rather than a comfortable prayer mat. He always kept a bag of bread in front of the shop door for poor people to take from freely without subjecting themselves to the humiliation of asking for food and the possibility of refusal. Over the years people came to know him as someone who would assist with whatever possible: money, a favour, a meal, or just simple advice. He employed his less fortunate relatives and treated them as equals. Those who would remember him years after his death would always talk about how he dealt with his employees as if it wasn't him who paid their salaries. His sons, who worked in the shop during their summer breaks, would remember countless occasions where people would show up at his shop door with requests of assistance, and keeping in mind that most of Mahgoub Gaafar's work of charity was done in secret, this would give them only a glimpse of his generosity. Once, a young man walked hesitantly into the shop in the middle of the day, with the story that he had been accepted into Gordon University, but had nothing more than the clothes on his back to take to the big city with him. Could he help? Mahgoub Gaafar loved education, and loved those who pursued it. Without further ado he took the young man by the hand into the market, and purchased for him a full range of clothes, suits and pajamas, along with the suitcase to pack them in, and sent him on his way. He felt just as much respect for that young man as the man had for him; because he had done him the honor of asking for his assistance alone, out of an entire village, and for such a noble cause.

But it wasn't just money, generosity and simply being nice that set Mahgoub Gaafar apart from his peers. It was something else, something that was of great value in a country that put so much weight on racial and tribal origins. He was one of the few who had astounding foresight and compassion, who saw the good in everything and everyone, and who recognized that home cannot be home if one does not work hard to build it. It started with a small science institute, followed by a high school for boys, then an elementary school for girls; the first in the area. Then a mosque here and there, and the rehabilitation of a small dispensary unit, and then a children's ward in the first local hospital, in which worked the first officially trained midwife, whose education and training he had funded and overseen himself. Along with his knack for successful business, Mahgoub Gaafar had inherited innate leadership skills, and the unique ability to rally communities around a great cause.

He recognized the importance of education at a time where education meant nothing except for the necessary ability to add sums to use in the market, and the basics of reading to help memorize the Quraan. Although he could afford to build entire schools himself, he insisted that everyone chip in with what they could, recognizing the importance of community participation to create ownership, and to instill the love of education in those who facilitate it. His love for education didn't stop at the borders of his own village, but extended even to the distant regional schools and their attached dormitories, as he funded the students' meals and allowances. He dreamed of the day a university would be built in Kareema that would be affiliated with the prestigious Al-Alzhar in Egypt. He encouraged people, both wealthy and poor, to work for their afterlife, and advocated for the building of mosques and Islamic libraries. For every new mosque built in the region, he promised and delivered the roof, and the hilal for the minaret. And he set his own shops and a collection of offices as endowments with which to finance those in need. Part of his trade was in the oil and gasoline business, and he was the official agent for Mobil Oil at the time. Farmers across the region would send their requests to him with the passing caravans, and he would measure out what they needed and send it back, without charge for those who couldn't afford it. Then, after several months, when the season's harvest had been collected and sold, the farmers would pay him back without interest. He also introduced modern irrigation techniques with machinery instead of the traditional manual methods, which helped farmers double and triple their production by saving time and effort. And he was the leading figure in introducing the water and electricity networks to the area, fighting for long years after almost everyone had given up, traveling up and down the country collecting donations and rallying officials, reaching all the way to the minister, until finally the first drop of tap water and the first electric light bulb was seen.

His children and grandchildren grew up in a prosperous and loving household, and each could swear that they were his favourite child from the way he treated them. They all received a fair education and grew up to be successful and leading figures in the country and a pride to their hometown. His most important accomplishment with them, however, was to instill in them the same compassion and love for helping those in need, even (especially) strangers. After almost 50 years of giving, he was finally taken quietly away, and was buried, as he had requested, between his older sister and his mother, in a simple and plain graveyard lying in the shadow of the great Jabal Al-Barkal. Just as he had lived his life in modesty, his death was just as so.

The ability to break down cultural and tribal barriers, and to give without humiliating, is what the people loved about Mahgoub Gaafar. When Nimeiri came to visit as president, a popular poet was asked to stand up and say a few words to honor him. He refused, and instead turned towards the short, bearded man standing next to him and delivered an intimate and beautiful poem, praising the well-loved man who had given so much and asked for nothing in return but good wishes and prayers of acceptance. Every house, every khalwa, every person in that region had been touched in some way or another by him, and he was thanked for it in his life and well after he died. And he was only one of many men and women that formed the essence of the Sudanese culture and history, and who would serve as an example of, despite everything, just how much good exists in our world.

God rest his soul.

About the author:

I am a doctor, writer and photographer, and blog at http://reemgaafar.blogspot.com. I grew up between New Zealand, Oman and Sudan, and recently settled down in Sudan to work in the civil service. I love reading and good food. I write mainly short stories but I am currently completing my first novel.

A Lake the Size of a Papaya Fruit
By Stella Gaitano
(FIRST PRIZE WINNER)

Everything in her reminded me of the huge papaya tree standing loftily at the center of our spacious house court: her tallness; her straight, age-defying posture. To me, grandma was utterly devoid of beauty; in fact I thought she was as ugly as a gorilla. She had thick lips and a head big enough to conveniently seat a full adult. Her lower lip was adorned with a huge hole that she had to plug up with a piece of wood carved specifically for this purpose. When she removed that piece, saliva dribbled uncontrollably. Yet the most popular feature of her ugliness was her pug nose. Whenever she was teased about this she would indifferently say: "At least it's good enough to help me breathe".

I could see the horizon through her huge ear hole that occupied most of her earlobe. There was another hole in her pug nose and a good part of her lower gum was exposed, thanks to the removal of four teeth. She had reddish eyes guarded by swollen lids.

Grandma had an amazing ability to tolerate pain. One day she went out to relieve nature and on returning she started to scrub her heel which began to swell up. There was nothing in her that suggested she was feeling any pain. When I innocently asked what was wrong she simply said: "Apparently it's a snake bite." She took a sharp tool and made a cut through her foot to bleed out the venom. She did that with amazing coolness, as if the sharp tool was making grooves in someone else's body, not her own flesh.

I grew yet more nervous on seeing black blood oozing out of these grooves, forming a black pond, a mixture of venom and blood. She then took a white stone, crushed it forcibly and then went about stuffing those grooves with the small stone fragments. All this happened as I vainly scanned her face for any sign to suggest she was in pain.

Suddenly she looked at me. I shrank back and racked my brain for an excuse to leave. I decided to run away because I was aware of her habit: whenever she took any medicine she would force me to take it as well so that infection should not pass on to me. Unfortunately, she managed to place her steel grip on my wrist before I could run away. She ran the sharp tool twice across the back of my hands and feet so swiftly I hardly had time to scream. I felt pain rampaging through my veins, then blood drops gushing out of the eight openings. She then took hold of her antidote and pressed it no less forcibly against my body, as if she were trying to literally insert the tiny pieces through my veins.

"Here you go," she blurted in a voice anything but feminine. "Now these moving ropes will not dare sting you. If they see you, they will freeze until you go away."

That was exactly what happened. Ever since, neither of us was stung by a snake though there were plenty of them everywhere, even in our spacious court, with its thick trees, vegetables, and the papaya tree with its big, numerous boobs.

Our room was built of thatch, had a rounded wall and a door so short that one had to go down on his knees to enter. From the entrance, three steps led down to the centre of the room. Only from there would the conical ceiling come to view high up. At the corner of the house stood a pen where over 30 cows lived. My nostrils were constantly invaded by the smell of dung, mixed with the fragrance of fruits and vegetables –and the smell of my grandma.

She and I were the entire family, a family composed of a grandma and a granddaughter. My mother had passed away while giving birth to me. My father had died during a hunting trip when a furious buffalo thrust its horn into him. My grandfather had been executed for murdering an Englishman, tearing his throat with a spear just because he didn't like the way the Briton looked at him!

So I lived with grandma from day one. She breastfed me up until I was ten. Her breasts were as huge as the papaya fruit, and I savoured the taste of their fresh milk. I would have a suck before taking the cows out to pasture and on return would be desperate to reach for the papaya fruit on my grandma's chest. I was eight at the time. One day she was not home when I returned. I started calling for her as I drove the cows into the pen. There was no response. Like a mad addict I started to call out loudly.

"Yes," her voice finally came to me from behind the ditch reed wall where she was sitting with our neighbour. "Are you back, my daughter?"

"Hurry up! I am hungry," I shouted, my throat narrow with rage, tears welling up in my eyes. She came back and sat on the straw mat. I grabbed on her breast ravenously, unbothered by the mocking of our neighbour, ridiculing my grandma for continuing to breastfeed me all these years.

Grandma wore nothing save for a two-piece leather drape dangling from the front and back to conceal her private parts, held together by a leather strip wrapped around her tummy button. Until that age, I couldn't understand why grandma had to put that veil on those parts, and wondered why she couldn't be just like me.

At the age of ten, I went through some transformations that changed my life. Grandma made me two leather slices to cover the same parts she was concealing. Another change: she discontinued the breastfeeding. I went through tough times, sleepless nights during which I had a compelling urge for breastfeeding and for going in the nude. I struggled for days to rid myself of those embarrassing feelings. Yet I never missed a chance to get back to my habit, particularly when grandma hosted drink parties with her aged friends. After those parties, grandma would be too intoxicated to feel my encroachment to my favourite papaya fruit. Yet it bothered me that after each such party, once her friends had left, she would start to talk to the dead. Addressing my mother, she would say: "You, Rebecca, my daughter: were it not for your fear of death in childbirth, you wouldn't have died."

"You Mario, it was your stubbornness that killed you, although you are not generally known for bravery."

"As for you, my beloved husband, what killed you was your ignorance."

She would then turn to me, her utterances getting even more blurred, her eyes redder and her lids swollen to explosive proportions, while her restless tongue pushed leisurely on the wooden piece that had become part and parcel of her flabby lower lip:

"Did you know how your grandpa died?"

"No, grandma."

In fact I knew that story by heart, yet I said no because she was going to narrate it regardless of my answer. Her tongue was getting heavier, words trickled out in blurred, cut off syllables, her voice sounded distant and vibrant as if her head was trapped in a big jar.

"Your grandpa had killed an Englishman during the colonial rule. The court sentenced him to death but the verdict was not communicated to him. Instead, he was instructed to deliver a letter to a certain destination far away. Your foolish grandpa was very happy because the British gave him the honour of delivering that letter. So he carried it, carefully wedging it in a ditch reed so not to get dirty. Upon arrival, he was accorded summary execution. Even death could not obliterate the perplexity that pervaded his stupid face."

She then burst into a hysterical fit of laughter. Then the same story would be related all over again, prompted by the same question. Clusters of blurred phrases and words would flow, with longer pauses between sentences, between words, and even between letters. After bursting into an equally hysterical fit of wailing, watering her chest, she would then plunge into silence, followed by heavy breathing which would develop into loud snoring reverberating around our spacious house.

At this point my heart would leap in excitement. Now I would be able to do what I wanted without fear of red eyes or a manly voice ordering me to go away. I would remove the leather cover and throw it away and approach grandma as she lay sound asleep, her limbs spread everywhere, even the two leather slices barely concealing any part of her enormous body lying on the floor of our room. I would grab hold of her breast and start sucking rapaciously. At the first suck, her nipples always tasted of salt, the taste of her tears. I was never nauseated by her ugliness because I loved her. I would cherish those moments as I listened to the thunderstorms outside and the persistent hits of the heavy downpour against the thatch roof. I would forsake all this clamour of nature in favour of my favourite world: a lake the size of a papaya fruit, a lake that grew so old that it began to dry up and to sag and droop down to the tummy button.

One day I was on her tail on our way to fetch water from the river. I was fifteen years old by then. We were following a narrow strait created by footsteps across the waist-high grass. She had on her head a big black jar which she held in position by her left arm, exposing armpit hair turned red by the scorching sun and sweat. I could see the horizon through her ear hole and could count the wrinkles on her face and discern other signs of aging in her stumbling steps, her flaccid tummy and breasts that now clapped against her belly as she walked or danced.

She was unusually silent and withdrawn and at times I had to trot in order to keep pace with her. Suddenly she halted on seeing a coloured serpent around which butterflies in matching colours flapped their wings.

"Since when would grandma stop at seeing a serpent?" I teased her.

She sighed deeply and for the first time I could see a combination of fear and sadness pervade the numerous, deep grooves in her face.

"This serpent is a bad omen," she said.

We went on, silently. Suddenly she said:

"Know something? I saw your grandpa a few days ago."

"In a dream?"

"No. In flesh and blood."

"But he's dead, grandma. How could you see him again?"

"I saw him, transformed as a crocodile."

Her stern look aborted my short lived teasing laughter.

"But grandma, how did you know it was grandpa?"

"On account of his famous limp – and other signs known to no one else but me. So I realised that we do not actually die but transform into other creatures that maintain our original attributes. The only thing we lose in transit is our memory. So your grandpa no longer remembers me now that he has transformed into a crocodile."

"And what is it that you want to transform into when you die, hopefully not anytime soon, grandma?"

"I don't know. Hopefully into an eagle."

Since grandma died, I have become deeply attached to eagles. Whenever I see one in the air, I follow it in earnest, hoping to catch a glimpse of my late grandma: a breast the size of a papaya fruit, red eyes, swollen lids, or salty breast milk.

Note from the author: This piece was originally written in Arabic, and was translated by the talented Adil Babikir, who was kind enough to do so for the purpose of this book.

About the author:

Born in Khartoum 17/11/1979, where I spent my schooling years until 2006, when I graduated as a pharmacist from the University of Khartoum. I have one published collection of short stories, 'Withered Flowers'. I am now working on a new collection of short stories and a novel (published in Arabic). Now I reside in my new home country, and work with other intellectuals toward building their burgeoning state.

MY SUDAN
by Rula Ghazal

"SUDAN OR SWEDEN?" I cried out, when my husband told me that he had decided to flee the country to carry our dreams for a better life to Sudan!

The trend at that time was to escape economic hardship at home; leaving behind your entire family, your dream house and childhood memories. Those days were filled with a bitter taste because of financial hardships and un-fulfilment of youngsters' dreams. In their minds, it was always greener outside the country.

Being a newlywed bride who lived with my in-laws and a post graduate student with no income, I was between two hard choices; either to let him go and discover that "other" world for our future life, or to make him stay to keep my bridal image in the society.

Soon I found myself at the bus station carrying his luggage, holding his passport and trying to hold my back tears as his bus, which was the only means of transport out of the country, was due to depart in 30 minutes. I could sense he was more worried than me for failing to achieve and succeed. After all, he had a one-way ticket.

"La ilaha ila Allah" were my farewell words to him and he answered *"Mohamed rasol Allah"*. As the bus drove off, all the hands were waving good-bye to their dear ones. Everyone was worried: will we meet one day again, will they be sent back from the borders for a made-up excuse from the border-guards, or will they be jailed for fleeing the country? I had faith, which kept me at peace.

Thirteen years later in Sudan, and now with my two children, I feel victorious. When I first arrived here, it was all foreign to me; the culture, the language and even my life. When pregnant with my first child, I had a hard time coping with both the pregnancy and the lifestyle. I craved soup and the only place that offered it was the Hilton Hotel and The Golden Gate Restaurant! My poor husband had to drive half an hour to get to either of them. After having two spoonfuls, I would vomit and feel satisfied! The roads were unpaved; in my condition I felt every bump in my back and that did not help me. Airport street was the longest asphalted road but had no pavements. The shops on each side were all called "Centres" with limited goods available and often expired. The Diplomatic Shop was considered an entertainment. All our friends would go during evenings to shop for soaps, automatic powder, creams, and shampoos.

Often we would stand for an hour chatting about "unavailable things"! It was a joy when we could find a newly delivered brand and it would be the gossip of friends who found them and hurried to tell the others. If I needed a needle to sew a torn skirt, or a ribbon to put at the edge of a shirt, or a plastic jar, or some cloth for a curtain, the only places that I could find such commodities were Al Suq al Shabi, Suq Umdurman or Suq Saad Qishra. Finding varieties was not part of the shopping process. Whatever was available in one shop would be similarly available in the other. We didn't need to shop around!

Having a cup of coffee or a slice of a cake meant going to one place only; Disney Ice Cafe. It was the best in town with an air-conditioned hall. Khartoum 2 Area Street was always crowded on Thursday evenings with cars stopping by for take-away pizzas from Pizza Hot. There was nowhere to sit. On the other hand, Sahiroon Hospital where I had my delivery was a 5 star hospital then. The VIP rooms had special staff and a high standard of service. I wasn't as satisfied when I had my second delivery in 2007.

Swimming was an activity that kept us busy and entertained during weekends. The International Community Club (then known as the American Club), was a meeting centre for Sudanese and non-Sudanese. We had our swim, lunch, afternoon tea and dinner there. The service and food were reasonable. I was happy to be a board member for one year.

My family and I went on a trip to Kassala during one Eid. We were amazed to know that hotels close during Eid! We ended up at a nice condominium that one of our Sudanese friends recommended. We had a passion to discover the area. We climbed Al Taka Mountain and had our jabana and popcorn. We contemplated the lengthy historical Mukram and Total. We also saw the Sufi Mosque. It was a memorable trip that mingled the ancient with the picturesque present.

Khartoum has changed immensely since then. Now when a place is referred to as a "Centre" then it is a Centre! One-stop shops can be found everywhere and international restaurants serving Indian, Thai, Mexican, Iraqi, and Syrian foods are well designed and filled with customers. My family enjoys spending leisure time bowling, enjoying Sega games, watching a movie at the cinema (mostly Arabic speaking movies) and rounding off the day in the fast food court at the oldest mall in town; Afra.

My historical experience in Sudan has expanded my knowledge. As a youngster, I learnt that Pyramids and the River Nile meant Egypt and only Egypt. Upon arrival to Sudan, I realized that this idea was a common misconception! I started to re-read about them and also decided to visit the Mugran, driving along the Blue Nile. It is a fascinating view seeing the confluence of the two Niles; the dark brown Blue river merges the silver White river. It looks like a sea meadow.

I consider my trip to the Merowe and Bajrawia Pyramids the trip of my historical reincarnation! Because I am fond of history and historical places, I was in a status of dreaming about how I might once have existed in that ancient time and place! Standing beside brick made monuments, even those unnamed, still made me shiver with "the greatness of that culture". It is the ruins, tombs, throne area, royal bathroom and temples of past civilization that remind us that the River Nile once flowed here. I am proud that I can talk and argue about this to anyone historically ignorant!

My life experience in Sudan is one of my life's merits. It has blended my family's personality and thinking. My family and I would sometimes be stopped at airports to be asked if we were aware that the plane would be going to Khartoum. My children's reaction would be "Yes we are going back home!"

I have tried to express this feeling in this poem:

The Dialogue of Cultures
My eyes welled up…
Seeing the embrace of the …
Calm White with the Rage of the Blue,
Since Pharaohs time till today,
The mighty Great Nile flowed.
Eternal as the Iraqi Euphrates and Tigris,
The two companion rivers,
Rippling softly,
Every day and night,
In the dark and in the light.

Oh ancient land of Merowe…
Thy pyramids exalt to visitors and walkers by,
And the Stones of Eastern Takka*,
Showing the world,
The symbols of the past and present high …
As great as Mesopotamia,
Glorious with Assyria and Babylon,
All other cultures rose after,
Isn't God the creator?

A Sudanese bride calling,
Ornated with tobe, henna and bakhour,
Dear people … share my joy,
In the merge of East and West,
In my North and South,
By peace blessed …
The Iraqi Mandili bride* answering,
They killed me on my wedding day,
But God achieved my dreams by you living them today...
So live and challenge…
For our children; our future generation of writers, scientists and artists,
For our husbands; the Land of the two Niles and The Ground of the two Iraqi rivers,
Each filled with everlasting waters
For our families; Iraqi clans and Sudanese tribes
This is the African Sudan of Arabia…
I am inhaling its dust in my years…
Long ago I have travelled away from my country's path…
And today am walking on Sudan's way,
I lived here …and I lived there …
My dreams will never go astray…

*   Takka- A high mountain in Kassala, East of Sudan,

*   Mandili Bride: Mandili is a border town between Iraq and Iran. A bride was killed on her wedding day due to an Iranian bombardment on the town during the Iraq- Iran war.

About the author:

My name is Rula Ghazal. I come from the Land between the Two Rivers; Mesopotamia, which nowadays is known as Iraq. I completed my Masters in Translation and Linguistics in 2001, from Al Mustansiryia University in Iraq. Writing has always been a breath of fresh air to my needs to express myself. It is not an easy process but the end product is self-satisfactory. Also reading in both the Arabic and English language is my favourite hobby and my haven at the end of every day routine.

Letter from Kassala: Cartwheels, Limes and Lionel Messi

by Sam Godolphin

Working in Khartoum brings with it many pleasures that one could associate with capitals across the world: a relatively good variety of restaurants, numerous cultural events, and a fair number of party invitations. However, as something of a 'melting pot' for the various tribes and peoples that make up the country, little of Khartoum seems to genuinely reflect what life in the regions of Sudan is like. I had not had too many chances to leave the Khartoum area since travelling to Ethiopia before New Years', so by February I was long overdue a trip away. I planned to visit Kassala for a few days in the middle of February, which happened to be exactly half a year after I arrived in Sudan. Over this period I felt I had become much more familiar with a country that had appeared so alien when I first arrived. Walking out of Khartoum Airport terminal building to be embraced by the uncomfortable warmth of the African night seems a world away. I now feel rather at home in what have become strangely familiar surroundings. It has become second nature to greet strangers in the street, enjoy tea with far too much sugar, and indicate that I want the bus to stop with a loud, assertive click of the fingers.

Kassala is a large town far in the east of Khartoum, a couple of hundred kilometres north-east of Gadarif, where I had stopped briefly on returning from Ethiopia. After a bumpy seven hour bus journey from Khartoum, we arrived in the out-of-town coach station and took a rickety bus to Souk al-Sha'abi (the People's Market) at the centre of the town. A dilapidated fairground – complete with a Ferris wheel – acted as a peculiar backdrop to the town as we approached Souk al-Shabi. It was noticeably much greener than Khartoum, El Obeid or any other part of Sudan that I had previously visited. This was strange, considering that the town's main river was dry for the vast majority of the year. However, we had heard stories about the dangers the river brought on the rare occasions it did have water; a few dozen people had been killed in recent years after the river burst its banks and flooded part of the town. We passed over the river, a stretch of dry, barren earth at least a hundred metres wide, banked on both sides by mango trees, lime groves and other greenery.

The town itself was cleaner than Khartoum, and appeared much more traditional, with the majority of men dressed in white Jalabiya robes (often with a waistcoat over the top) and virtually all women in various forms of Islamic dress. We stayed in a suburb a little way from the centre, in a one-room outhouse in a family home complex. Everyone we met was friendly and generous without exception, in a characteristically Sudanese manner. Farmers let us take photos with them and encouraged us to explore their lands, full of banana plantations, guava orchards and horned cattle lazing about in the relentless mid-day heat. One particularly welcoming group of herders gave us water, lunch and a massive bag of limes. Hours of exploring through various fruit orchards followed, with an awkwardly large bag of limes in tow. It was a simple plastic bag, filled to the brim. Inevitably, some fell out as we progressed, leaving a little trail behind us reminiscent of some Sudanese version of a Brothers Grimm tale. Inshallah, this will become a trail of fully-grown lime trees one day. The remaining limes ended up becoming a gift for our delightful hosts.

The old part of town, Khatmiyah, is famous for containing the tomb of Seyyid Hassan, one of the first Sufi Muslim leaders to come to Sudan from Saudi Arabia to spread his religion. His roofless mausoleum sits next to a ruined mosque: complete with neat rows of intricately-carved pillars, but strangely missing any form of roof. Sufism is known for its tolerance and acceptance of outsiders, and we were able to spend a few hours exploring this site. Individuals and groups were seated in the shady sand around the tomb itself – an unusual combination of holy men engaging in meditation and prayer, and young boys (presumably Islamic scholars) laughing as they cartwheeled in the sand together. We later made our way to a floodlit café complex at the bottom of Totil Mountain, which seemed particularly popular with honeymooners. We were told that the floodlights had been installed a couple of years ago to prevent couples creeping off into the rocks to enjoy themselves. I have no idea how true this is, but the coffee was great and the location was very impressive. One could not help but imagine the temptations that the dark, welcoming rocks would present to a newly-wed couple enthralled by passion and slightly high on caffeine.

The scenery was like nothing else I've seen before. Khatmiyah had been built at the foot of a mountain range which rises almost impossibly steeply above it, with some little rural communities living literally at the base of the rocky incline of the Taka, Totil and Aweitila mountains. During one memorable incident, we were taking a shortcut through one such community, where we attracted the attention of local children. They crowded around, laughed and threw questions at us – some in broken English, some in Arabic, and others in local dialects that we had no hope of deciphering. My limited experiences in such situations have taught me that football is the great global connector, potentially capable of bringing London-based British graduates and Eastern Sudanese infants together, so I discussed the various merits and drawbacks of Lionel Messi, Neymar and Cristiano Ronaldo with them in broken Arabic. More and more children would appear from the surrounding houses, glancing shyly around doorways before plucking up the courage to join their playmates. They seemed enthralled by the bizarre manner and appearance of these peculiar strangers. One can only guess as to who they thought we were and where we had come from. When we eventually left, they chased us down the road – these kids who had grown up in the shadow of the mountain, who somehow thought WE were the exciting ones.

About the author:

Sam Godolphin is a 24-year-old British MA graduate who has been discovering life as a 'Khawaja' in Sudan for the past nine months. Sam is currently working in universities in Khartoum as a volunteer English lecturer in collaboration with the Sudan Volunteer Programme.

A BRITISH TEACHER IN NEWLY INDEPENDENT SUDAN
by Gareth Griffiths

It was 1961, I was 29, married with two small daughters under two. I was teaching Geography in a secondary school in UK. I already had experience of Africa doing my national service and I felt the need for change. I started applying for posts overseas. Amongst my applications was one to Sudan and I was called for interview at the Sudan Embassy in London. I have no great memory of the interview but at the end I was told that they would let me know whether I had been successful, and sent me off for a medical examination at an address in Harley Street. The medical was held in most palatial premises; I was ushered into a commodious waiting room, equipped with a silk dressing gown and then shown into the surgery of an imposing elderly doctor.

After the medical he said, "Well, my boy, how do you feel about going to Sudan?"

"They haven't accepted me yet," I said.

He chuckled and said, "My boy, if they are paying my fees, they have accepted you."

He was right and a few weeks later I took a Sudan Airways flight to Khartoum. No one met me at the airport so I took myself to the Grand Hotel and booked in. The Grand Hotel was grand in those days, wide corridors, verandas overlooking the Nile and, though it now seems hard to believe, the room and all meals cost two pounds and fifty piasters a day. The next day I had a long walk along the Nile to the Ministry of Education where I was told that I would be posted to Juba Commercial School in the south of the Sudan. By the time I returned the following day the Naib of Khor Taqqat had been in to the Ministry, exerted influence, and instead I was to go to Khor Taqqat.

The train journey to El Obeid was scheduled to take 16 hours. I doubt that this was ever achieved. It took me two days to travel to El Obeid, a long journey but the record for journeys to the school was held by Rod Usher, who arriving two years later, took a week to get from Khartoum to El Obeid. The facilities in sleeper class were most comfortable. What detracted from the comfort was the fact that one either had the windows open and received a cool breeze and was covered in dust, or kept the widows closed and sweated. The dining car served bland traditional English food. It suited me but as I was the only non-Sudanese in the dining car, I was the only one suited.

Khor Taqqat was the third of the major secondary schools that had been set up by the British. Each was located near an important centre of population but each was built a considerable distance from the centre of population to deter the students from engaging in political activities. Wadi Seidna was about eight miles outside Omdurman; Hantoub was the other side of the river from Wad Medani; and Khor Taqqat was about eight miles outside El Obeid. After the intermediate schools' examinations were finalised, the top 600 boys from the whole of the Sudan were sent to these three schools: the boy who was first went to Wadi Seidna, the second to Hantoub, the third to Khor Taqqat, the fourth to Wadi Seidna and so on until all 600 were placed. This meant that the students in these three schools were the cream of the cream: all were highly intelligent. I subsequently taught in a British university but never after I left Khor Taqqat did I teach such intelligent pupils. In addition, almost all were hard working. They had to be. They had been taught English in intermediate school, but in secondary school all subjects apart from Religion, Arabic and History were taught through the medium of English. It could be argued, and doubtless was, that it was not right that the language of instruction should be a foreign language, but it certainly resulted in the level of English of educated Sudanese at that period being exceptionally high. Certainly when a few years later the language of instruction in secondary schools switched to Arabic, there was an immediate drop in the standard of English.

I was a Geography teacher but I found that in addition to teaching Geography, I was to teach English Language and English Literature. In one way, teaching in Khor Taqqat was easy: teaching bright, hard-working pupils is easy. But there were difficulties. English Literature did not present me with any problems. The set books were a Shakespeare play (I think it was *Romeo and Juliet* in my first year), a novel (I think it was *Youth & Gaspar Ruiz* by Joseph Conrad) and another modern play (I seem to remember *An Enemy of the People* by Ibsen). These would be challenging texts for first language speakers but they were understood and appreciated by my Sudanese pupils. I remember the odd tear when reading certain parts of *Romeo and Juliet* – Sudanese men present an outward macho image but can be quite sentimental. My problems came with English Language and Geography. I was not a trained teacher of English as a second language. I knew correct English but I did not understand why what was correct, was in fact correct. In addition, formal grammar figured in the syllabus for School Certificate. However, there were text books and I had to undertake a speedy and steep learning curve with grammar in that first year. The biggest problem was the Geography: physical geography was fine; climatology was OK; natural regions of the world gave no problem; I had always been good at map reading. But the regional geography of the Sudan was another matter altogether. I knew that Sudan was the biggest country in Africa; I knew it was wet in the south and dry in the north; I knew that the Nile ran through the length of the country; I didn't know much else. I asked for a text book. No text book. Panic! I found a weighty volume called "Agriculture in the Sudan" that had been published about ten years before and managed to prepare some lessons from this. Then I heard that the professor of Geography at Khartoum University was publishing a book on the geography of the Sudan. I air-mailed off to the UK for a copy. No reply. I air-mailed again and thus received two copies. I was saved. Actually I only taught Geography for the first two years. For the remaining eight years I was in Sudan I just taught English.

Teaching in Sudan was very different from the UK. In the UK, I was lucky if I had three or four free periods a week; in Sudan I had twenty. When not teaching in Britain, the only facilities were in a crowded communal staff room; in Sudan I had my own desk in a roomy office. The school day in Britain was nine to four; in Sudan work started at 7.30 then there was an hour break for breakfast which I found to my surprise was a social meal, then school finished at 1.30.

Family responsibilities were viewed differently in British and Sudanese schools. When my younger daughter was born at home in Britain, there were no family members nearby and I had to stay at home to take care of my 13 month old elder daughter while my wife was giving birth. The school stopped me a day's pay for my absence. Fast forward nine months: my family was arriving by sea at Port Sudan. The headmaster insisted that I went to meet them to accompany them back to the school. This took 14 days: no pay was stopped. What a difference.

In addition to the actual teaching at Khor Taqqat, there were boarding house duties and it was expected that staff should support whatever games were going on in the afternoons and help with prep in the evenings. It was a good life. I was reasonably well paid; the teaching was stimulating; I had a pleasant house on the school campus; I had time to spend with my young family; I enjoyed the company of the boys I was teaching. Looking back, I think it was probably the happiest time of my life.

There was a cadet corps at the school. This was enjoyed by a few but was unpopular with the majority, as was the military government that existed in Sudan at the time. Secondary students had been a political force when the British had been in Sudan. They continued to be a political force. There were differing political beliefs; the Muslim brothers and the communists were at opposite ends of the political spectrum but most groups came together to show their opposition to the government by going on strike. Strikes happened about once a year and followed a predictable pattern. The students would demonstrate in the town and the school, and would then be sent home. After a few weeks, angry fathers would bring their recalcitrant sons back to school. The leaders of the strike would be expelled. The remainder of the students would be beaten by the army sergeants of the school cadet corps. Beating 800 boys was a long job and the sound of beating, which resembled carpets being hung on a line and thumped with a stick, would last all day. I was on occasion asked by my students if I would beat them instead of the army sergeants. I don't think that this was because they thought I would beat them more gently, it was that they found being beaten by the sergeants to be degrading. I never found myself able to accede to their requests even if the school would have allowed it, which I doubt. I can remember discussing an imminent strike with one or two of the student leaders. They knew the pattern of strikes; they knew that as leaders they would be expelled; they knew that they would probably never get to university as a result. Their argument was that they thought what they were about to do was the correct thing and that they could not live with their consciences if they did not carry it through. I admired their stance but I thought (and think) they were wrong.

In my first year at Khor Taqqat I taught Geography, English Language and English Literature to Third Ghezali. In my second year they became Fourth Ghandi and again I taught them the same three subjects. In addition I was their Abu Fussell. As the name suggests this is a more important role than the equivalent British form master. In addition to teaching them I supported them in the various sports competitions. Each year they invited me and my family to the form picnic, which involved a lorry, a live sheep soon to die, a fire, shady trees and usually custard. They were entertained in my house; they knew my children. At the end of my second year I said goodbye to thirty five boys wearing the school uniform of khaki shorts and white shirts. Of the thirty five, twenty obtained places at Khartoum University – a high proportion. At the end of my third year when I got off the train at Khartoum to go on annual leave, I was met by twenty tall young men in snowy white jallabiyas and ammamahs who whisked me off to a tea party at the university. I couldn't have been happier.

About the author:

Born South Wales 1932. Lived early life in and educated in England. Worked as teacher, lecturer, teacher trainer and inspector in England, Nigeria, Northern Ireland, Sudan and Oman. Retired to a life of idleness in 1996 first to rural West Wales, now to East Anglia.

The Patient Ones
by Elizabeth Harrison
(HONOURABLE MENTION)

"And when he attained to working with him, he said: O my son! Surely I have seen in a dream that I should sacrifice you; consider then what you see. He said: O my father! Do what you are commanded; if Allah please, you will find me of the patient ones."

Quran 37:102

Even with the flaps pinned open, the tent is oppressively hot. I shift on the rope bed biting into my backside and feel sweat trickle down my spine. The sheer folds of my gauzy *tobe* stick to my arms and neck, though miraculously it still refuses to stay put on my head. To my left, nestled in the back corner of the tent are a few household goods – a charred pot, several tea glasses, clothes in a basin. To my right is a triangle framed view of the camp – troops of half-naked children playing in the cleanly swept dirt that borders the UNHCR tents and bare-ribbed huts all clumped together like an unnaturally gathered crowd. In the foreground, Om-Iman's husband and a couple of other men sit on *bumbars* drinking coffee from porcelain cups cradled in the sockets of their palms as they rest in the thorny shade of a *lalob* tree. I envy their proximity to fresh air. But Om-Iman must stay inside for now. So we sit with her.

I notice the other women in the tent with me have let their tobes pool in garish puddles around their waists leaving their arms bare and their heads free. Relieved, I shrug mine off too. The difference is slight but welcome. Aisha, sitting directly across from me, our knees nearly touching in the small space we inhabit, is wearing her old leopard print tobe that I know so well. She was wearing it the day I met her, back when we both lived across the border. A neighbour who had heard I was looking for house-help brought her up to my front door and introduced us, hovered nearby briefly and then left us alone together in uncertainty. I had walked her through the house and showed her where I stored the basins and broom and where I kept my plates. I didn't know any Arabic back then so our conversation was stilted and awkward, relying mostly on gestures and the only moderately helpful use of facial expressions. But even then her smile, half embarrassed and half mischievous, put me at ease and made me feel like she understood my words, whether or not they were spoken in a language she understood. Whether or not they were even spoken out loud.

During the first few weeks of her employment we would sit on the back porch, her leopard print *tobe* hanging limply from a low rafter overhead while she perched on a *bumbar* and leaned over a basin, her arms white with soap suds; I sat on the half-wall, legs dangling like a school girl, and hastily scribbled down new words in a cheap notebook covered with the off-laid image of some European football star. And we talked. At first about the price of bananas in the market or the ages of her children. And then, as the weeks turned into months and the language gulf between us began to narrow, we talked about whether or not her husband had been drinking that weekend, whether or not I would ever have a baby, if war would come again.

As it turned out, war did come again. We all scattered in the wake of the bombs, me on a Cessna caravan that never even turned off its engines, her on foot through the bush. We met again over a year later, here, on the other side of the world's newest international border. The *tobe* was one thing that she had brought with her. I sometimes wonder what other things she has from her former life, but have never asked her.

I don't know the woman sitting on the bed beside me. Her *tobe* is olive green with gold embroidered geometric patterns around the hem. I am guessing it was once expensive but it is threadbare now and the ends are frayed. Aisha has just introduced the woman to me as her sister though I know all of Aisha's immediate family members are in a camp in Ethiopia. I wonder if they are in fact related; are merely sisters in another sense. They don't look alike. This woman is short with thick braids woven into her scalp. She wears an expression like someone gazing at something troubling on the far horizon, her brows knitted with intensity. But despite the reason for our gathering I have already heard her burst into loud laughter twice, a sound that catches me off guard. Her arms are thick with muscle and lined with raised scars. Her name is Limon.

Om-Iman sits on the bed across from us, next to Aisha. She is Aisha's closest neighbour, a woman I have met only in passing, once or twice at the market buying oil, several times sitting on a mat outside Aisha's house. Until this afternoon I have always assumed that she is the mother of a child named "Iman" and is thus called by her firstborn's name. I have only recently discovered my mistake.

She is not wearing a *tobe*, only a thin cotton nightie that says "Love nice lucky girl" with a rhinestone heart stamped on the front. On either side of the heart wet stains are slowly blossoming like dark flowers against her breasts. I realise with a sting that the milk must be dripping down her empty belly.

Aisha is speaking to Om-Iman in their shared mother tongue, tangy nasal words that sound to me as dry and unfamiliar as the chalky baobab fruit the children eat out of the tree at the edge of my fence. Beside me Limon is nodding fiercely. My ears ache to understand. Om-Iman is looking down as she brushes the back of her hand across her flawless obsidian skin, each cheek etched delicately with small crosses. The crosses shine beneath her tears but she doesn't make a sound. The strand of black and white glass beads hanging around her neck pulses slowly in the hollow of her throat as she controls her breaths.

I can't help but notice that Aisha does not touch her. There is no hand holding, no conciliatory pat on the back. But glancing down I see that the two women's ankles are resting slightly against each other on the dirt floor, one over the other, like a tired woman in the throes of labor bracing herself against a sister's shoulder. In this moment I also notice a scar on Aisha's shin, taunt and shiny like a puddle of dark wax. I remember one of our afternoons on my back porch in years gone by and scraps of a story play at the edges of my memory. It was shrapnel, I think. But where had she been when she was hit? And how old was she? Who took care of her? I try to remember, but can't.

I am pulled back into the present by the sound of Om-Iman's voice. She is speaking in Arabic now, and looking up I realise she is talking to me. "The first time I delivered the baby alive but she was too early. She only lived for one day. She was my *bikir*, my firstborn." She says these words calmly, casually even, and I simply nod. "The second and third times there was only blood. So much blood. But this time," she pauses, "This time the baby was like this…" She holds out a slender arm with her palm outstretched and encircles the space a few inches below her elbow with her hand.

I briefly wonder if the baby has already been buried, and if so where. Was there any kind of ceremony? Or did this child quietly join so many others before him and slip under the still surface of death with no fanfare or fight.

"Om-Iman … I am so sorry. So very, very sorry." The inadequacy of my words burns my throat.

She looks at me and I am startled by the unexpected softness in her eyes. I feel weighted by our mutual awareness of my general lack of suffering, as though she can see the prenatal vitamins casually sitting in my bathroom cabinet threatening to go out of date, the bush pilot's number tucked away in my phone for any emergencies, the dark blue passport sitting in the go-bag in my closet that will get me easily across most borders. But her eyes hold no judgment. She holds my gaze as she says steadily, "It is the will of God. He has asked us to be patient in this life. I will be patient. I know he sees. He sees everything does he not?"

Her words hang in the air around me and I savour them, testing their authenticity. I roll them in the palm of my mind seeking out their definitions. I find them heavy with pain but the rough grain is smoothed over with a grace and resilience that rings like truth.

There is a stirring at the entrance of the tent, and a short woman with a baby tied on her back enters carrying an aluminium tray that clatters pleasantly with coffee paraphernalia. Limon shuffles to plant the plastic table between us firmly on the soft floor and the woman sets the tray down. She spoons small mountains of sugar into the *finjil* placed in front of each of us and then pours a steady stream of rich, black coffee from the burnished clay *jabana* into each one, miraculously filling each to the perfect brim. I raise the small cup to my lips, more slowly than the others as I manage the heat in my fingertips, and feel a rush of pleasure as the scalding coffee burns my mouth with sugar and ginger.

I watch my hosts as we drink together. The mood is shifting, I can sense the lightening as we drain our cups again and again. Om-Iman has stretched back into Aisha and is leaning absently against her in a way that neither seem to notice. They are listening as Limon reenacts the story of killing a snake that came in under the door of someone's tukul at night while everyone was sleeping. I don't catch if this story is recent or from long ago, but it clearly involves people they all know and the women shriek with laughter. The rope bed sways as Limon beats the air with an invisible stick. Aisha covers her mouth and squeezes her eyes tightly shut as she is overcome with hysterics.

The woman who serves us coffee is sitting on a *bumbar* near Om-Iman's feet. She was introduced to me as Om-Iman's co-wife when I arrived an hour or so ago. I have already forgotten her name. I was surprised to find out that Om-Iman is a senior wife. She still seems so young and beautiful. But I confess to knowing little of the complexities of marriage and fertility, love and youth, war and responsibility in such a place as this. They sit together easily, like old friends.

The woman has taken the baby off her back, a girl only a few months old, and is nursing her. I can't help but see that the woman's breasts are covered with raised dots, perfectly symmetrical scars that look like carefully flung constellations on her skin. They rise and fall between the splayed fingers of the nursing infant. I have never seen scars like these before. I wonder how old she was when she got them, who gave them to her.

When she finishes nursing she passes the baby to Om-Iman and rises to clear the table. Om-Iman takes the child and bounces her lightly over her knees, her long fingers playfully drumming on the baby's bare back. I search Om-Iman's face but see only white teeth and a pink tongue stuck playfully out at the baby. Her pain is tucked somewhere out of sight, somewhere close beneath the simple joy of smooth baby skin and milky hiccups.

I watch these women around me, women close enough to touch. I hear their voices – long sighs, soft laughs, tongues clicking heavily with disapproval. I smell the coffee on their breath. I see the sweat shine in bright beads on their foreheads. I know their stories, at least a few of them. Some stories from years gone by, others I have only heard a few heartbeats ago. Stories of loss and pain, survival and deep disappointment. And yet in this moment as I look across at the women around me I feel a deep and inexplicable envy.

Like the raised crosses and dots etched into their flesh, there are scars in hidden places that unite them in an even deeper sisterhood than I can imagine. They carry on their hearts the marks of a more intimate tribe, a more select clan whose price of membership I will never be forced to pay. Aisha leans down to brush an ant from Om-Iman's foot – her hands are still full of another woman's baby – and Limon finishes a joke about her mother-in-law. And all of this happens seamlessly, as though none of them can see the cloud of sorrow hanging over this small tent as blinding as the harsh blue sky outside.

Perhaps someday I will be able to speak to them in their mother-tongue and not just mingle in this middle ground language we all navigate with only moderate skill. Maybe then I will better understand all the nuances of their laughter. Maybe someday I will stand beside Aisha as she lays her firstborn in the hard earth and watch as the small wrapped body is covered with sand. I pray that someday I will sit with Om-Iman at the *asimaya* gathering where a sheep is slaughtered to celebrate and praise God for the gift of her living healthy baby. Should those moments come, I will be welcomed into them with more grace and hospitality than I ever deserve. But my loud trills of overflowing joy will not be the ones holding up a mother's heart spilling over with thankfulness. And my deepest animal wails will not be those that help carry the grief a whole community must bear together in order for anyone to survive under its crushing weight. Alone in my security, or at least my highly developed illusion of it, a part of me will always long for the beautiful thing these women share that I would never wish on another human being.

The sun is sinking towards the dusty horizon and it is time for me to go. I give my final words of condolence and Om-Iman holds my hand in both of hers as she thanks me for coming to visit. As I rise to leave she stands, shakily, and pulls a basket out from under the rope bed. She pulls a speckled pumpkin from its rusty bed of sorghum and presses it into my hands. "You are my guest, please. You must take it."

Aisha walks me to the main road. She shoos away the throngs of children trailing in our wake chanting "*Khawaja, Khawaja!*" and then laughs as they boldly ignore her. We stop to say goodbye one last time and I hoist the pumpkin on my hip as we grasp each other's hands. She reminds me that she is coming by my house later in the week so that she can teach me her language. I tell her I will have the coffee ready. We squeeze each other's hands one last time and then she turns to walk back towards the tent, her leopard print *tobe* blowing dramatically in the hot wind as she slowly moves away. I watch her for a moment and then carefully cradling my gift, I turn and walk home alone.

About the author:

Elizabeth Harrison has been in the Sudans since 2009 working in the area of literacy. She loves tobes, scalding mint tea, listening to people's stories and watching her two small daughters tear into plates of kisra.

Illustration by Mutaz Mohamed

THE GOLD MARKET
By Dan L. Lukudu

"Lokule, you better not be dressed like that," said Johnny, my older cousin. "A tucked-in new shirt and a new pair of blue Edwin jeans - no one dressed that way can come out of that market without being victimized."

"No, no ... that's not true," I argued, shaking my head. "Nobody can ever pickpocket me, if that's what you mean. I'm twenty ... you know. It's the elderly who've lost their senses."

"My advice is - look casual and you won't attract attention."

"Don't worry. I'm old enough to take care of myself."

And off I went to the Omdurman Popular Market, in search of the best deals on sports boots.

———

About an hour later, as I alighted from the bus and crossed the street, in the blazing Omdurman midday heat, I was not surprised to find the market so overcrowded. The hustle and bustle was as far reaching as the street, at least ten metres away from the market square. A distinct and tantalizing aroma of spiced Shaiya, or Shawurma, emerging from a restaurant nearby, filled the air, as I headed towards the stalls. Several vendors stood in the uncomfortable heat, behind their displays of various produces and other items. One man had a heap of ripe brown dates in front of him, and he kept calling out "Fresh dates! Sweet dates! Come buy the best dates ... dates, dates, dates!"

I passed the dates-seller and a few other vendors.

When I reached a stall, next to another middle-aged salesman, I had to slow down, as the customers ahead of me appeared to have stopped moving. In front of the salesman, on the ground, was a large canvas sheet on which was a heap of grain - wheat. Next to this, were a bushel and several measuring cylinders. The salesman, dressed in a white jallabiyah, stood there addressing passers-by: "Famine ... famine. All over the radio ... famine, the TV ... famine, the papers ... its famine. Come people! Buy now! Tomorrow I won't be coming, for famine is coming ... so fast it's coming!"

"Which radio?" asked a grey-bearded man.

"Omdurman radio," replied the salesman.

"How come I didn't hear that?"

"That's the latest. You must've missed it!"

And then the salesman started again: "Famine, famine, famine. Radio Omdurman says famine ... famine, famine. If I were you, I'd buy everything, for famine is coming, so fast it's coming!"

Looking on, a broad smile appeared on my face. And I was not the only one. I noticed a number of people with happy faces, while they too stood listening to the trader.

The salesman must have noticed me smiling, as soon as some customers cleared the area in front of him. "Sharp-looking young man ...," he said, "I'm sure the family needs some grain?"

I shook my head and started moving on, still wearing the smile. To me it was always fun listening to such salesmen, cleverly attracting customers. And I had often wondered about how people like him are so persuasive.

I brushed past another slow traffic of customers - young and old, male and female, who were constantly stopping to buy or inquire about something.

As I left the row of stalls and strode to another, a short distance away, I heard a voice calling from behind me.

"Excuse me! Excuse me Mister!"

I turned to see two boys hurrying towards me. One was shorter, and he appeared to be in his mid-teens, while the other stood taller - about six feet - and looked almost my age. The younger one was dressed in a knee-reaching, white jallabiyah, while the other wore a nondescript shirt and a pair of dark trousers. Both youngsters had flip-flops on their feet and their appearance looked unkempt.

The pair stopped when they reached me.

"Are you looking for anything in particular? Maybe we can help," said the taller teenager, with a light-brown complexion. "Anything ... gold, whatever –."

"No," I cut him short, while shaking my head. Then without any further thought, I turned to move on.

"Wait ... mister. Maybe you want the best deals. We can help."

"No." I walked on.

They followed me, trying to convince me.

I ignored them.

Then they melted in the crowd.

A short while later, just as I was walking towards another group of stalls displaying metal utensils and colourful plastic-ware, two other teenagers came hurrying towards me. Their looks, except for their clothing, which was a shirt and a pair of trousers, in both cases, was no different from the others I had encountered a short while ago.

"*Ya seyyid*, interested in gold?" One of them asked.

"No," I replied.

Then the other produced a shiny, golden bracelet from a side pocket. "You've no idea what kind of opportunity you are turning down," he said. "Look, this is half-gold. We can sell you pure gold for the lowest price."

Just what were these guys up to? I asked myself. I thought of ignoring them, but then a sense of curiosity within me overruled that decision. Perhaps these were the swindlers and thieves about whom I had heard before. If that was how they did their dirty work, then let me find out. "And what's your price for the pure gold-bracelet? I asked, pretending to show some interest.

A smile crossed the youngsters brown face, and he signalled me to follow him towards a shop, some fifty metres away.

As we approached the shop, I saw three other boys, whom I assumed to be in their mid to late teens, standing next to a small tree that would not have survived the heat had someone not been caring for it, with tap water from a green hose.

The trio came forward as they saw us walking in their direction.

"Show him," said the youngster whom I had followed. And I began to wonder whether that was a pre-arranged meeting.

One of the three produced another shiny golden bracelet, from a pocket. He took the other bracelet from the teenager I had met earlier, and placed them side by side. "You see the difference," he said." What I have is 99.9 % gold."

The bracelets looked the same; instead of inquiring for a proof, I asked, "What's your price?"

"How much can you offer?"

I assumed it was a question to test my knowledge of the pricing. "I can't say. You're the seller ... name your price," I replied.

"For you alone," he said, revealing a double row of yellow teeth, "I'm offering just twenty thousand pounds."

"Twenty-thousand pounds! That's about seventy dinars. It's more than twenty plates of the common foul

... in any of those restaurants." I indicated in the direction of some food joints by the roadside.

"How much can you pay?"

"I say ... seven."

"That's an insult." He turned, pretended to walk away, stopped, and returned to face me again. He then added, "Nobody can sell you such gold for less than half the price. This is quality. It's from the Nubian Desert. It has blessings of the ancient kings. He paused, and quickly glanced around, then said, "I'm giving you one more chance. Just one more chance!"

"Twelve," I said.

"Afta-allah!" he said, and repeated his moves. He then said, "Seventeen!"

"Thirteen," I said. And suddenly I realized I was in the middle of all five boys, two facing me and the other three seemed to be arguing behind me. I felt unsafe and decided I had to find a way out of this.

"Fifteen," said the young man.

"I actually did not come for gold," I said, suddenly. "Besides I still find it expensive."

I turned and started walking. At that moment, I realised that the other three boys were out of sight.

"Twelve. Take it!" said the teenager, while following me; then he stopped.

I ignored him.

"Eleven!"

I kept on walking.

When I was a few meters away, I turned to see the two youngsters hurrying away. I was glad for having left before it was too late.

Hurriedly, I walked towards a less busy path between another rows of shops. I was hardly five metres in the path, when I saw a young man, who looked a bit older than me, about to cross it. He was dressed in the common *jallabiyah*. Murmuring something to himself, he glanced twice behind, before stopping a few feet away, facing me.

"Mister ... want to buy any gold?" he asked.

"Gold? No! No!" I said, almost stuttering, as I shook my head and walked away. At this point, I began to wonder what it was with the gold, and why everyone was approaching me with it. It was then that I decided to head to another market.

I hurried to the bus stop and immediately got into a departing mini-bus. I did not buy what I came for, but as I finally took a seat, I felt a sense of relief, escaping the "gold-sellers." I'll never go back to that market, I thought to myself.

Before long, the bus conductor approached me. He snapped his fingers, motioning me to pay my fare. When I dug my hands into my side pocket, it was empty! Desperately, I searched all my pockets for my wallet, and felt blood rushed to my head, when the thought of having been robbed engulfed me. It was then that I shouted at the top of my voice: "Quick ... stop the bus! Stop the bus!"

END.

Endnote

Afia-allah – a common phrase used by traders when haggling, especially when they don't agree with an offer, and they would like the customer to make a better one.

Foul – fava beans/ broad beans: a popular dish in the Sudan.

Jallabiyah – a thin loose robe, usually white in colour, common in the Sudan.

Saiya – roasted meat

Ya seyyid – a respectful way of addressing a male unknown to you. In a way, it is similar to "Sir".

About the author:

Dan L. Lukudu was born in Juba, in what is now South Sudan. He holds a Master's degree in Drug Discovery, from University College London and a Bachelor's degree in Biomedical Laboratory Research Science from Rotterdam University. His interest in Creative Writing arose from a culture of reading, since his school days. He has aspired to write like world-renowned authors, whose work he has admired for so long. He has used writing contests, reading and independent research, to perfect his writing skills.

Illustration by Hussein Merghani

AHMED SUK SUK
by David L. Lukudu
(SECOND PRIZE WINNER)

"I must eat a decent meal today!" Ahmed Suk Suk said to himself, as he woke up and sat on the bed. "I haven't had some warm food with salt in days," he lamented. "Yesterday, it was just some miserable *kisra*[1], a leftover from a neighbour; scrambled with sugar and this water that one can get freely everywhere, even from the grand river – the Nile!" He shook his head gently, and then sighed deeply: frustrated!

He had slept in a police cell four days earlier and was whipped the next day and then released, as required by law, since he was caught drinking. He was with two others. And they were killing the hours with *aragi*[2], in broad daylight, at Kapuki's secret bar here in New Mayo, on the outskirts of Khartoum, when the police struck. He could not recall what happened to his money – wages amounting to two months– that he was carrying with him in an 'inside' pocket, before the surprised raid and arrests. Maybe the cash fell in the boozer during the scuffle with the men in uniform; perhaps he used it unknowingly to buy more drinks for his friends, as the rounds kept spinning; or, maybe, it dropped in the police station. He might never know. That meant for him a search for another workshop to weld together metal pieces to earn more money. After absence of two days from his work place, without warning, he knew he had lost it this time. It had happened twice before, and each time it was alcohol-related, with police arrest. But of course, he did not say this to his employer. But the boss knew. Nonetheless, the big man was kind enough to give him a last chance. Should he repeat the careless act, he was cautioned, he should consider himself fired!

"Whatever!" Ahmed Suk Suk said to himself again. "I'll survive, God willing … But today, I must eat food worth eating!"

He was a first class welder, he believed; coming a long way. Before he got to Khartoum, he was Satimon Lujang in the South, living in Wonduruba, with hardly any skills: felling trees for charcoal, and tilling the soil! He had started out here as a construction labourer for years and had a hand in the erection of various structures: banks, bridges, hotels, and other buildings competing in the skyline across Khartoum; and he was proud of that. Next he drifted into the industries: soap, vegetable oil, soft drinks, etc. Then he peddled chick peas: boiled and salted and packed in tiny plastic bags; he attracted children as he shuffled along in some neighbourhoods, a bucket dangling from his hand while he cried out: "*Keb-kebe! Keb-kebe!*" … Chick Peas! Chick Peas! … But soon he became a milkman; he manoeuvred a donkey cart and penetrated one suburb after another. Later, when he discovered welding, he leaped into it; with no plans for a turnaround.

He got up, slipped his feet into a pair of flip-flops, and adjusted the knot at the waist of his baggy, knee-length and once-white-but-now-faded boxers. Next he toddled to the door of his mud-walled and box-shaped shack. He pushed back the bolt and stepped outside. Then he picked by the door a plastic kettle containing water and washed his face in the open while bending. He also rinsed his mouth a few times with the aid of a finger, spitting the water on the ground each time; before heading with the container to the latrine in one corner of the mud-walled compound.

When he was done with the toilet, he strolled back to his room. Inside, he shuffled to his suitcase in one corner, squatted and rummaged through the case, and picked out a white *jallabia* out of three: the one that looked less dirty. He stood up and put on the robe, and then sat on a plastic chair. After that he squeezed his bare feet into a pair of simple, hand-made, leather-like shoes that were close to the chair. A rotten smell, which he knew was coming from the footwear, hit him in the nostrils, but he cared less about it. He got up from the chair and retraced his steps to his suitcase. He bent and picked out a white scalp cap and adjusted this on his head.

He walked to a pair of trousers hanging by a nail on one wall, searched the pockets scrupulously, and found his keys. He also found 25 piaster – coins.

"This can only buy sticks of cigarette, or sweets for children," he complained to himself as he slid the change into a pocket.

He strode outside, locked his door and the gate, and then marched to a dirt road that linked his area to the tarred road to the city centre.

Maybe he should finally cease this intractable habit with the endless and surprising police raids, he reflected. The arrests and the lashes he had witnessed several times and fallen victim to more than once were becoming unbearable. Or perhaps he should move out of New Mayo altogether, with all the temptations of the environment, he digested further. What's more, didn't a doctor warn him about his liver, only three months earlier? The doctor explained to him everything and instructed him to stop drinking. But still he could not understand himself; even two years after the split with his wife!

He spotted Marco, a neighbour, who lived on the next block of mud-walled and box-shaped houses. Marco was with his wife and two older children; the family loading mattresses, suitcases and boxes onto two hired donkey carts, probably heading to the main road to catch up a bus to the city centre, from where they would take another bus southwards to Kosti town at the border, to connect with a steamer to Renk and then Malakal in South Sudan.

He slowed down and waved: "Marco! Safe journey!"

The neighbor paused, looked at him and shouted back: "Thank you, Ahmed Suk Suk! Stay safe!"

"Thank you!"

He walked on.

Going back to the South? Well, he loved that place because that was his home of origin. However, he still had no prospects of joining the exodus back there; he had been assuring himself of late. He had witnessed countless South Sudanese, like Marco, packing up their belongings to head back home after so many years in the North. From where would he start? He wondered. He was not sure if he could easily secure a welder's job in Juba. Still, he had no piece of land there. Furthermore, he heard that life was expensive and rent was a nightmare! Twenty five years here in Khartoum, then all of a sudden the country ripped into two, like a loaf of bread split in the middle! Just like that? He wished the Sudan remained intact and continued enjoying the status of the largest country in Africa. He never liked politics and yearned people everywhere tried to come together instead of breaking apart and drifting away from each other. He loved it here in Khartoum: the affordable life; the tangible progress he had witnessed and contributed to; the brotherhood amongst the people; the politeness; the generosity; the security. Khartoum and Sudan had given him so much over the years, and he was not ready to part with both. Not yet!

He arrived at Yasin's shop, where he regularly bought cigarettes and other items. The proprietor was alone.

"Good morning!" He said.

"Good morning!" Yasin replied.

"Brother, I need a loan, please!" He said immediately, a solemn look on his face. "I'm not feeling well today."

"Well, business is bad these days," the shop owner said. "Besides, how much do you owe me in Sudanese pounds?"

"Haj Yasin, I promised I would pay you; how can I forget!"

"Well, I'm waiting!" The shopkeeper shrugged and started to arrange items on the shelves, appearing to be busy.

"I'll come back then," Ahmed Suk Suk said, and turned and walked away on towards the paved road – disappointed.

He stood by another shop: Suleiman Kadugli's. He saw numerous customers at the counter and hesitated. Moreover, again, he owed Suleiman Kadugli: about five weeks of his wages! He had a feeling nothing positive this time would come out of this man from Kadugli.

He trekked on, yawning deeply, his jaws threatening to dislocate, and he felt his stomach growl, like he was suffering from some diarrhoeal illness. He was not sure if he could find any restaurant operational this early.

He reached the main road and stood for a short while, like someone lost. He recognized fruit vendors already by the roadside and gazed at cars and pick-ups zoom back and forth, as well as donkey and horse carts clip-clop along.

"It can't be like this!" He said to himself as he walked on along the wayside.

He yawned again and crossed the road to another shop he was familiar with. At least he did not owe Abdel Muneim anything, as far as he could remember, not even a piaster. He could see only two consumers at the counter.

"*As-salamu alaykum!*" He said.

"*Wa-alaykum s-salam!*" Abdel Muneim and a buyer said simultaneously.

"Can I borrow a plate, *alek* Allah[3]?" he said. "I'll bring it back in about 20 minutes."

"Sure!" Abdel Muneim said and picked up from one end of the counter a metallic bowl, medium size.

"Thank you!" Ahmed Suk Suk said; a smile on his face. "God bless you! God bless your children, and your children's children, and the children of your children's children, and the children of the children of your children's children!"

"Thank you!" The shop owner said, and then added: "You'll need to wash it."

"Not your problem, brother," Ahmed Suk Suk said, as he brushed off with his fingers the dust and food crumbs in the container. "It's clean enough."

"Remember to bring it back; it's almost 10 o'clock."

"Twenty minutes!" Ahmed Suk Suk said.

"Twenty minutes!" Abdel Muneim repeated.

Ahmed Suk Suk moved ahead to the next block of buildings.

He felt beads of sweat form on his brow, despite the low heat this early, and wiped his forehead with a hand.

"I must eat a decent meal or something closer today!" He reminded himself.

He reached a bakery. He was surprised to see someone who he thought looked like Dunia, a one time friend, at the counter.

"Dunia!" He called.

The man looked at him with container in hand.

"I'm not Dunia," the man said. "There must be a mistake."

"There's no mistake!" Ahmed Suk Suk said. "You must be Muhammad then."

"Wrong! I'm not Muhammad either!" The man's tone was business-like.

"You mean you're Ibrahim, or Musa, the one I met in Omdurman, or was it Suk Al-Arabi?"

"No! I'm neither Ibrahim nor Musa! Don't even try Ismail or Omar!"

"No worry, brother," Ahmed Suk Suk said, a quick smile on his face. "Do you have fresh bread?"

"Yes!"

"Is it the white one," he said, "the best quality, made from the best wheat around, the long one, like this limb of mine?" He raised briefly his right forearm, holding the bowl with his left hand.

"Yes, we have that!"

"Allah is Great!" Ahmed Suk Suk uttered, raising a hand upwards, momentarily. "That's why this bakery has a good reputation in this part of Khartoum."

"For how much?" The other man seemed to be getting impatient.

"Please, brother!" Ahmed Suk Suk pleaded; "Just give me the dried pieces! The unsold and damaged ones you dry to preserve, the pieces you sell at a cheaper price. No cash on me today, *Alek* Allah!" He held the bowl with both hands in front of him, his face deeply sincere this time.

The man behind the counter looked at Ahmed Suk Suk from head to toe. He noticed the scalp cap, the seemingly swollen face and lips, the dry mouth, the rumpled and dirty *jallabia*, the old pair of simple shoes, and then said:

"No problem; you can have that." He hurried into a room at the back and emerged holding in front of him between his two hands a load of dried bread pieces of varied sizes and shapes.

"God bless you!" Ahmed Suk Suk said, as he held the container firmly in front of him and the man poured the pieces into it. "God bless your children, and your children's children, and the children of your children's children–"

"Thank you!"

"And the children of the children–"

"Enough!" The bakery man interrupted. "I have customers ..."

Ahmed Suk Suk turned and quickly walked in the direction he had come from, a full smile on his face.

He crushed the longer pieces of the bread by pressing them with his thumbs against the bottom of the bowl, tossing a tiny piece into his mouth, as he retraced his path.

He reached Abdel Muneim's shop. He saw there were no buyers.

"Abdel Muneim!"

"Yes!"

"I told you I would be back in twenty minutes."

"Yes, you did."

"Exactly twenty minutes!" He looked at his left wrist, as if looking at a watch, though he had none, while the container rested on his right palm, and he smiled, adding: "Don't you think I'm a trustworthy person?"

"You're a man of your words? What's your name again? Ahmed Sukkar?" Abdel Muneim could not hide a beam on his face.

"No! I'm the one and only Ahmed Suk Suk in this neigbourhood!"

"My bowl?"

"Sincerely, Abdel Muneim, your broad beans must be ready now," Ahmed Suk Suk said, turning his head away from the counter towards a stove on one side at the front of the shop. "I can sense the aroma, and I can see the steam jetting upwards from the cauldron, like from a chimney in one of the best hotels in Khartoum."

"Yes, the broad beans should be ready," Abdel Muneim said; then got out of the shop and walked to the stove and giant aluminium pot outside.

Ahmed Suk Suk followed.

"Is it the best quality; the light brown and giant variety; the most delicious?"

"Why not?"

"Can I have a look?"

"For how much?"

"Open first and I see ..."

"But how can you see with the steam?"

"Didn't you hear about Ahmed Suk Suk's extraordinary eyes?"

Abdel Muneim could not control his smiles. He opened the top of the container quickly, using a piece of cloth, and waited for a short while for the emerging steam to settle; and then grasped a ladle hanging by a side handle with one hand, took the bowl from Ahmed Suk Suk with the other hand, and repeated:

"For how much?"

"Brother!" Ahmed Suk Suk said; "Please! Just give me the water. Not even a seed of beans. I'm broke today. Just the water! *Alek* Allah!"

"Al-laaaah ..." Abdel Muneim grumbled; but then went on and scooped a few ladles-full of the hot, brownish water from the cauldron onto the dried bread pieces in the bowl.

"God bless you!" Ahmed Suk Suk said, as he watched the proprietor pour the hot liquid into the container in a circular motion. "God bless your children, and your children's children, and the children of your children's children, and the children of the children of your children's children!"

Abdel Muneim handed the bowl to him without uttering a word and hurried back to the shop to attend to a couple of shoppers.

Ahmed Suk Suk followed.

When Abdel Muneim was done, Ahmed Suk Suk said:

"Brother, please that white cheese, the salty, Sudanese-processed, the one you were giving that young man a little while ago; just the water! *Alek* Allah!"

The shop fellow shook his head in displeasure, his face expressionless. Nevertheless, he grabbed the bowl from Ahmed Suk Suk, turned to a large rectangular tin on his side of the counter, and using a tiny plastic cup he kept in the tin, poured into the container the light, milky liquid above the cheese blocks.

"And just a pinch of this– Please!" Ahmed Suk Suk said, as he seized the bowl, and then picked a pinch of rough salt crystals from a heap in a plastic basin right in front of him.

"Suit yourself."

"God bless you!" Ahmed Suk Suk said; then supported the container on his belly with one hand and sprinkled the salt crystals onto the contents with the other, adding: "God bless your children and your children's children–"

"Yes, yes, thank you!" The shopkeeper disrupted him. "You can go now and have your breakfast outside there."

"Thank you!" He bowed slightly, his face beaming, but only briefly.

"Just remember my container."

"Yes, I haven't forgotten!" Ahmed Suk Suk said. "But I'm not done yet!"

"Oh yes, you're done!"

"How can a Sudanese have a meal of broad beans, especially *boash*[4], without oil, Abdel Muneim?" Ahmed Suk Suk said. "Do you have the popular, Sudanese-processed, yellowish, and fine quality sesame oil?"

"Oh yes, Ahmed Suk Suk! I have the popular, Sudanese-processed, yellowish, and fine quality sesame oil! But you forgot one thing?"

"What's that?"

"There's no water this time!" Abdel Muneim's face was serious, and he was shaking his head and waving an index finger in front of him to emphasize his point.

"Yes, of course, I know that!" Ahmed Suk Suk said, as he deepen his right hand into a side pocket, holding the bowl with the other hand, and removed the few coins he had; "Give me the popular, Sudanese-processed, yellowish, and fine quality sesame oil for 25 piaster – only!"

End Notes

Arabic/Arabic slang translations:

1) Kisra – Thin, flat Sudanese bread usually made from sorghum

2) Aragi – Strong spirit made from fermented dates

3) Alek Allah – By God's grace …

4) Boash – Popular Sudanese dish; basically, jumble of boiled broad beans, bread chunks, white cheese bits, salad (usually tomato, onion, cucumber, rocket and green pepper), boiled egg cuts, falafel fragments, vegetable oil (sesame, preferably), and salt

About the author:

David L. Lukudu is a South Sudanese who has lived in Uganda and Kenya for years. He is a medical doctor who seems to love the pen more than the stethoscope. He has published with the BBC Focus on Africa magazine, AuthorMe, sudaneseink.com, Warscapes, McSweeney's Quarterly Concern, and the Guardian.

Illustration by Mutaz Mohamed

SPECULATIONS AND LESSONS LEARNED
BY THE AVERAGE SUDANESE DIASPORA CHILD
by Haneen Mohamed

1) every motherland occupies a space within its children's hearts regardless of whether one realizes it or not. love for your motherland is an unconscious and sometimes intangible love. you try to scrub traces of it off your skin and ease into a universe of denim and vibrantly colored sneakers, but you remember that when you enter your incense scented dwelling that your dark-complexioned fingers are told to resemble that of your aunt, a woman who is the protagonist of many intimate family tales, yet an abstract concept to you. you remember that like many sudanese women she was told to have loved fiercely and purely and it dawns upon you that it is hard to discard your roots when the lines on your palms remind you of the way the blue and white nile meet to form the sovereign river that eventually empties itself into the mediterranean sea.

2) you think you are an introvert until you arrive at khartoum's modest international airport where you are smothered with greetings and kisses and an unadulterated admiration that you didn't know existed. you are not used to spirited laughs and boundless smiles and you then realize that you have been brought up in a hemisphere where only silence thrives. you resentfully compensate for years of blandness and monotony by laughing louder and smiling unmindful to the crookedness of your teeth and you let your inner extrovert shine through. you realize that solitude doesn't come in handy as much as you think it does and appreciate the value of company. you learn that tasaali isn't any type of food but a food meant to accompany conversation and laughter. tasaali becomes an emblem of sisterhood and friendship.

3) one can think of arabic as a flower, each delicate petal representing one of its colorful dialects. a petal for the liveliness of egyptian arabic; a petal for the sentimentality of syrian arabic. but nothing amounts to the petal that symbolizes the vernacular of those who carry the elegance of elaborate toubs and radiant jalabiyas on their backs. sudanese arabic is a story telling arabic. sudanese arabic is an arabic erected with caution so that it accommodates the histories and secrets of the land with eloquence so that even gossip between neighborhood women and the shouts of street vendors sound poetic. there is no feeling comparable to letting every intricacy of sudanese arabic effortlessly roll off your tongue while eating mangoes with loved ones after sunset.

4) those who take off elsewhere always leave pieces of familiarity behind but it seems as if the land's rhythms and melodies are always the exception. the harmonious sounds of mohammed wardi and osman hussein never cease to fill the air during silent car rides and dull, rainy weekends. it is as if there were never a departure from home. like a mother, sudanese music acts as a remedy to despair and incessant worries. there is something reassuring about the strums of ouds and the energetic beatings of a dalooka. it dulls the aches of distance. it is no wonder your father protects his cassette tapes like a newborn child.

5) gaze at the lines on your palms and the daintiness of your fingers and remember what it means to carry the weight of your mother's land on your fragile shoulders.

About the author:

Haneen Mohamed is a German born, Sudanese-American residing in Saudi Arabia. Growing up in a country where identity is reduced to the contents of a "Race/Ethnicity" checkbox, she has spent a lot of time reconciling between identities. She is a Hip-Hop culture enthusiast and an anxious Secondary school student.

GREETING KHALTU FATMA
by *Mohamed Fakhreldin Omer*
(THIRD PRIZE WINNER)

I live outside Sudan. I have for most of my life. This brings with it the one thing I look forward to most on my calendar – the yearly trip back to visit my family. I think about all the smiles and all the laughs that will take place around the dining table. The classic, home cooked meals on which I was raised, which invariably contain a fistful of diced onions that have no business being there. I'm not a fan of onions, but I endure. The obligatory desserts follow which are usually too sweet; yet we don't hesitate to gorge ourselves on the flans and the cakes and the fruit salads. We're familiar with diabetes.

Then come the rounds, the visits to relatives in far off corners of the city. Negotiating the streets of Khartoum is a master class in heartrending vehicular encounters and near misses, requiring precision and patience of the highest order. All this set to the tune of a cacophony of car horns. At these moments I'm thankful that I can't drive. Even if I could, I don't know what I would do without a Sat Nav to guide me, given the Sudanese penchant for omitting road names from directions. Unfortunately, they might refer to a tarmacked road the same way I might refer to Oxford Street.

Seeing my family fills me with affection I can scarcely describe: my grandmother's eyes, my younger cousins' chuckles and a home littered with family photos.

We usually travel in December because the weather is pleasant and the wedding season is in full swing. All the family gathers on these happy occasions and creates happy memories. It is at these weddings I happen upon the downside of living abroad. The trouble with being away from my home country is that I did not come to know my family as well as I might have wished. It often makes me quite sad to think about it, not helped by the interrogatory encounters with which I'm regularly faced when meeting some of them at such gatherings. The series of exchanges is all too familiar; beginning with the jab that is a snide comment upon my Arabic, followed by a body blow snatching the breath from my lungs when they ask that dreaded question. Do you remember me? My answer…silence.

My heart beats faster and beads of sweat begin to form. I find myself divided, equal parts embarrassed and irritated. These are my elders and my blood but what do they know about me other than who my parents are? I would guess little more than I do of them.

In that one moment, with that question, my happiness abuts sadness. It wasn't my fault that I didn't grow up around them. I've met them as many times as they have me, yet they can tell me no more than my name. The tension I feel stifles any attempt at conversation I might otherwise conjure.

On one such round I visited my great aunt, Khaltu Fatma, in Bahri with my mother. She had gone for a gathering with her cousins and I went along to greet my relatives. Khaltu Fatma's bungalow sat on the side of a long stretch of road, solitary with no structures on either side of it. The sloped cement driveway covered in sand extended to the edge of the road, inviting would-be visitors to park up and enter. A plain exterior, nothing set it apart from any other buildings in sight.

Upon entry, however, something changed. There sat faintly familiar furniture which had remained a permanent fixture throughout the years, amongst which my relatives prayed and upon which they sat and confabulated over what sounded like a never-ending series of inside jokes, linked to their ever intertwined childhoods. My mother was instantly swept up in the atmosphere and taken back to what felt like a golden age in her mind. I couldn't help but feel enthralled by the warmth, and beam as I reached out my hand to greet my relatives.

But suddenly, that infamous panic spread throughout my body as my mother's cousins asked me that question and, once again, silence. Punctuated with twisted mouths. Silence. Rolling eyes. Silence. Loosening grips. Silence. Averted gazes. Silence, broken by a scornful comment about how I didn't know them, they didn't then tell me who they were. They seemed ashamed. I felt embarrassed again.

And then I saw my aunt, Khaltu Fatma. Her eyes lit up when she saw me. I immediately rushed over to her and embraced her. She kissed me lots and I hugged her back and then she looked at me and kissed me some more. She held my hand tightly and sat me down next to her. Then she tried to communicate but I didn't understand. She cried.

Her tears reminded me of the first time I visited her after her stroke, when she first lost the ability to speak. It was the first time I had seen her in almost a decade when I was a small child, so I had no real memories of her. She cried that day too, and I remember feeling a dull ache form in my throat. I didn't want to cry in front of her. I didn't want her to think it was her fault, that the sight of her was upsetting. I saw the struggle of a woman with a mind filled with wonderful memories, brimming with emotions and no adequate way to express either.

On the day of the gathering, I sat next to her and took her hand and held it. We smiled at each other. I apologised for not coming earlier and said I was busy with all these weddings, that Baba's side of the family doesn't have anything else to do but wed. She laughed. I asked Mama to take a photo of the two of us. We posed and smiled.

She didn't care whether or not I knew that she was my grandmother's sister. She didn't care that I didn't know who my mother's cousins were. She only cared that she knew me. She remembered me greeting her and hugging her at my sister's wedding a year earlier and taking pictures with her then. She remembered me kissing her hand on that day; I know she remembered this because it's what I remembered. She couldn't say a thing but she conveyed what was important and made me feel happy and made me feel connected. Her grip on my hand was surprisingly formidable, as though in that clasp she was summoning all her love and all her memories to be passed between our two hands, touching.

She exclaimed in angst when I said I had to go. I couldn't say I would be back soon. I just had to go.

The experience remained and recurred to me every day until the day came I was to leave Sudan. I found myself sitting in the departure lounge, having navigated my way through the bureaucratic pandemonium that is Khartoum International Airport. I wondered why it had had such an impact on me and as I did, a gentleman came and sat down beside me. As he introduced himself to me, I feared what was in store. Was he minded to make casual chitchat with me? Or perhaps request that I carry something to London for him?

He began by greeting me and, noticing my slight bewilderment, he acknowledged that I didn't recognise him. He did not recoil, he did not judge; he simply went on to explain to me our connection. He began by telling me who I was; my name, my parents and my relatives. The detail was quite impressive. Though this confrontation may sound bizarre, he in fact made me feel at ease. He then gave me his name and began telling me the location of our last meeting, sparking my memory into motion until I found myself completing his sentences. We delved into engaging conversation, sharing thoughts and experiences, which ended only when our flight was called to board.

As I took my seat and made myself comfortable, I contemplated why this conversation had been different. I thought about Khaltu Fatma and how she had made me feel. In the end, I guess what is said does matter. But what isn't said can matter just the same.

About the author:

I am 24 years old, currently living in London. My background is in poetry so this was my first story. I'm very happy to have been able to write something about my great aunt and I'm proud to be included in this wonderful initiative.

A Funjan Full of Sudan
By Amal Osman

The smell was so strong and delicious, it transcended into my dream world. I awoke with a smile on my face and a nose tingling with the aroma of burning bon emanating from our garden; *Haboba* was making the customary afternoon jabanah. I jumped out of bed, and slipped on my sifinja, ready to dash across the garden to the veranda which was located beside our kitchen, separate from the main house. I must catch it all while it's hot: the *jabanah* and conversation.

I found her sitting on her customary *bamber*, the various instruments to make *jabanah* balanced on a small table by her side. A circle of *bambers* surrounded her, almost as if they too, gathered to hear Haboba's mid-afternoon chatter.

'*Sabah al-kheir ya* Rashida! I thought you would never wake up from your nap. Come, your *jabanah* awaits you…' Haboba exalted, as she saw me approaching her. I took a seat on the sturdy *bamber*, wincing as some of the frayed pieces of rope rubbed against my bottom, cutting through the light material of the jalabiya I bought so many years ago in *souk* Omdurman.

'*Shukran* Haboba.' I replied.

I popped my head in the kitchen, surprised not to find my auntie there preparing for dinner. Though it would not be served for hours, she tended to spend most of her afternoon preparing for the meal of the day – the one where the whole family gathers around the wide aluminium dish used to balance the various dishes of fuul, kisra and mullah wekka, the chopped cucumber and tomatoes hidden underneath a canopy of spinach that my father can eat up within minutes on his own. I laughed at this to myself, remembering the flash of annoyance on my mother's face every time my father would do so.

I place myself on a *bambar* beside Haboba, watching her as she grinds more coffee beans for the *jabanah*. I don't need to ask her, I know she is making it just the way I like it – fresh, strong and so sweet I feel an instant rush of energy to my system, jolted by the richness of the beans and the company of my beloved grandmother. It's less then five minutes before my special *jabanah* is complete and she hands me my small *funjan* brimming with sweet steaming hot coffee. I take a sip and feel the warmth of the coffee beans, the warmth of my grandmother, the warmth of Sudan pass through my system. I laughingly tell her she must have put some of her soul into this cup because it is so good and rich, just as she is in spirit. Her hearty laugh fills the sweet air as she tells me it is only as good as the one drinking it. She tells me she will teach me how to make the best pot of jabanah there is, so I can catch the best husband – a handsome engineer, or better yet, a doctor.

"That's how I caught *Jidu* Hassan you know; he heard about my beauty, and when I made him my cup of *jabanah*, he couldn't resist me – it was a wrap from then. Don't you know a way to a Sudanese man's heart is through a good cup of *shai* or *jabanah*?"

"Ha! I don't doubt that at all Haboba considering the amount of tea and coffee everyone drinks here. No wonder everything takes so long in this country, everyone is always going off for tea breaks!"

"You young ones are always in such a hurry! Always fussing, always anxious – that is why Sudan is the way it is now, nobody stops to appreciate each other's company any more, to wonder at the magnificence that is Sudan and its various peoples. Not the way they used to…when I was a young woman, this country was thriving, and we still had our 6 cups of *shai* and *jabanah* a day." She replied with a wink and a crooked smile.

Nostalgia was in the air, and so I stayed silent waiting until she made her presence more felt. I looked up from my little cup at my grandmother to see her eyes swimming with distant memories of her younger years here in Sinnar. I could see the stories, the history on the tip of her tongue…

And so I waited.

I waited for the stories of my grandmother in her youth, enchanting, wildly attractive and intelligent.

"You know Rashida, when I was younger…"

She had begun. I sat back with a smile on my lips, a full *funjan* of *jabanah* warming my hands as the rest of me was warmed by my grandmother's memories.

She tells me stories of how Sinnar used to be a thriving city, full of businesses owned by the people of Sinnar. How the roads used to be so clean and people never dared to litter or dirty the streets of their beloved land. Sinnar used to be the capital of Sudan once upon a time – the Sinnar dam was a spectacle everyone came to see, it was the greatest sign of progress. Now, the rundown dam is only a haunting memory of past splendour and brilliance.

She tells me how it was my grandfather's quiet and humble nature, so very different from the other boisterous and quite arrogant men who had approached her before, which had attracted her the most. I imagine my grandfather standing proudly in his crisp white jalabiya, the 'ima looped so intricately and perfectly on his head, almost as if it was a snake that coiled itself upon him rather than the delicate piece of white material donned by the men of this land. I imagine him standing proudly with his hand stretched out to welcome the woman with the wide chocolate brown eyes, light brown skin, and hair which sparkled red under the sun – my grandmother, his wife.

She gushes about how tradition has changed so much, even from when she was young. How for her wedding celebrations, she danced the *ragees al-aroos* topless and in front of men! I couldn't imagine such a thing to happen in Sudan! In the Sudan I grew up knowing, the *ragees al-aroos* was in an extremely private and guarded setting, usually a large enclosed hall, full of female family and friends, with only one male allowed to be present… the groom!

She tells me stories of my aunties, her six daughters, and the numerous suitors who passed through the house with the hopes of marrying one of Hassan Al-Mahdi's daughters, known throughout Sinnar as the most beautiful, most intellectual, and most charming girls in town. Sought after by many yet very few succeeded in their attempts at wooing my aunts, but more importantly wooing *Jidu* Hassan! I laugh remembering how hard to please my grandfather it could be, and pitied the poor men who were turned away and deemed unworthy as future husbands for his daughters.

She tells me how my mother used to be in her adolescence, getting her hair done at Khaltoo Fatma's hair salon down the road, hair styled in a beehive fashion which was the craze in the late 60s. I suddenly remember a photograph of my mother and some of her school friends standing side by side, dressed in flowing white *towbs* with their hair elegantly coiffed on their heads. When I first saw it, I remember thinking they looked like empresses with their shimmering caramel skin brightened by the golden rays that fell on Sinnar. Haboba continues to tell me about my mother and her rebellious years; stories and memories I could go back and remind Mama of, showing her we weren't so different. Though she was raised under the shadows of the lemon tree which stands in the middle of my grandmothers yard, and I amongst the grey and towering buildings of London, we weren't so different.

As she speaks, I absorb her words, projecting the scenarios she describes in my mind, visualising life as she once lived it. In this moment, life is sweeter than the *jabanah* Haboba brews.

My mother always asks me why I love spending so much time with her mother, why I insist on staying a month in Sinnar with my grandmother instead of time in Khartoum with my aunties, even though my holiday is a month and two weeks. I tell her I'm catching up with History, Tradition, and Heritage. In between her stories of Jidu, of suitors, of my aunties, she tells the story of Sinnar. The stories etched into the dry reddish sand of this land. The stories of the people who colour the mighty Nile, giving it its brownish tint. The stories of those who pause under the majestic lemon tree, seeking solace from the unwavering sun, whose hopes and worries are absorbed by the branches that are keeping them cool.

I gaze at my grandmother with her *towb* bundled around her waist and knees; a powerful wave of admiration and wonder washes over me. It occurs to me how much she has lived – and how much of my love for this land – the land I have never inhabited, but always felt like home, is alive in her.

The motherland – Sudan – is you Haboba, mother of mothers.

Arabic/Sudanese slang endnotes:

funjan – a small cup the coffee is drank from (the size of an espresso cup).

bon – coffee beans

Haboba – Sudanese word for Grandmother

jabanah – coffee

sifinja – flip flops

bamber – small and round chair, similar height to a stool.

Sabah al-kheir – good morning

jalabiya – traditional garment native to people of the Nile Valley.

shukran – thank you in Arabic.

fuul, kisra, mullah wekka – Sudanese dish of made of cooked fava beans, sorghum crepes, okra and and sometimes minced meat finely blended and seasoned

Jidu – Sudanese word for Grandfather.

shai – tea

'ima – long cloth used to wrap a turban

Ragees al-aroos – a traditional celebration in a Sudanese wedding where the wife dances for her husband. There are various outfit changes. The music is supplied by a single drum and the sweet voices of relatives who sing the songs passed down through generation to generation.

towb – traditional native garment worn by the women of Sudan.

About the author:

Amal Osman is a literature student studying in the UK. Though raised in London, she visits Sudan yearly, where she finds comfort and a sense of home tucked in the folds of her grandmother's colourful towb. She writes to capture the moments and stories special to her, so that they may live long after she does.

Illustration by Hussein Merghani

A Northerner's Perspective: 'When my brother left!'

by Khabab Osman

I cried inside! Weeping tears of regret
Months and even years after my brother left!
Like a neglected sibling, un-favoured by our heavy handed father
For me it was hard, but for you it was infinitely harder
You probably resented my passive ignorance
As I hid behind the couch and watched him bruise your innocence
Without aiding in your resistance.
I stand only as your reluctant witness.

When my brother left! When my brother left!
He took a part of me with him
The heat from my grin, the melanin from my skin,
The belt from my waist, the shoes from my lace
I look forward in disgrace
As the cracked mirror reflects my broken face
Like the horizontal fault line that now divides our fates
Imprinted on me like a pomegranate stain
Ingrained in me as a reminder of from where I truly came
Your were closer to me than my jugular vein
Draining blood, like the Niles drain a vast terrain
Destined to meet once again
In the very place that drove you away.

When my brother left! When my brother left!
He was brave enough to leave, and that I respect.
Not knowing what comes next? What to expect?
Like a bird on its first flight from it's mothers nest
Like a diver exploring unseen depths
Like a Sailor in search of new beginning on his red sea quest
I pray you ride the storm beyond the ocean's unrest
All I can do is pray! And wish you the best
But brother!!!! I can't accept you left!

About the author:

Khabab Osman is a doctor training to be a surgeon. He was born in Sudan, but was raised in London and resides there still. When he finds the time to put down his surgical instruments, he picks up a pen, to master the art of poetics.

THE PENKNIFE
by Gabrielle Papin

You drive down the few tarmacked roads and you stop as young girls march in full regalia, all flowing fuchsia-lined black gowns complete with mortar boards. It is the last thing you would have expected, a surreal sight in a country where three in four girls do not go to primary school.

I have just arrived in Juba, a year after South Sudan became independent and a year after my father's death.

Everywhere, motorbike taxis, the main form of transport: boda bodas carry one, two or three passengers – or furniture. I spot one with a broken motorbike strapped horizontally at the back. The men fold their impossibly long legs around their machines. Some of the tallest people in the world are bent in half in tiny minibuses covered with faded Chinese characters.

He had only travelled abroad a few times, to neighbouring countries, for his military service in Germany after the war, then to see my sister in Spain and to stay with me in London. He had dreamed of visiting Ethiopia and there was one people he felt a kinship with: the Dinka.

The capital city of 350,000 has no traffic lights, no signs and just a few pedestrian crossings. Zebra can still be found two hours away, but not for long: US wildlife experts say they will disappear by the end of the decade, together with elephants and giraffes, if nothing is done to fight poaching. Some 300 wild animals are reportedly killed everyday in various parts of South Sudan.

My father had worked with cows all his life: as a boy and, later, as a young man, on his parents' farm; when he had got married, he had looked after a herd on the family's other estate; and, when he had rebelled against his father's authority, he had joined the local milk board, driving around to collect samples and advise owners on ways to improve the quality and quantity of the milk their cattle produced. He was fascinated by what he had read about the Dinka, partly because of the importance cows played in their lives: they drank their milk, washed their faces in the animals' urine, gave them away as dowry and ate them in times of famine.

Wildlife may be disappearing in South Sudan but compounds favoured by expats are proliferating. More are being built in the Western style, albeit with traditional, wooden scaffoldings. Until recently, most mud huts in Juba had a thatched roof and you could tell where wealthy people lived because they had a tin roof: they could buy barrels of cooking oil imported from the US, cut them up and flatten the cylinders to add to the patchwork. Today, satellite dishes can be seen protruding from corrugated iron shacks.

Generators are ubiquitous but many work sporadically. Some hotels boast round-the-clock electricity. A fellow journalist tells me he spends his days off out with his friends because, he says, there is no point staying at home as there is no power. He does not have a

TV or a computer. In the absence of land lines, sales of mobile phones are rocketing. There are no mains so tankers deliver water. Other companies collect sewage.

Piles of rubbish were removed on the occasion of Hillary Clinton's visit in August 2012. They have since reappeared. The streets of Juba are littered with discarded plastic bottles, a fallout from independence, some say: the bottles were introduced in the capital by returnees and the NGO workers who have come to live here since July 2011.

Most of the fruit and vegetables on display at Konyo Konyo Market are imported from Uganda. Only foreigners and well-off locals can afford to go to the handful of supermarkets where a weekly shop - tinned fish from Britain, milk from the United Arab Emirates and South African breakfast cereal – will set you back 200 South Sudanese pounds, the equivalent of a teacher's monthly salary. Everyone else relies on street vendors and corner shops. The government says more than half the people live below the poverty line.

Rice and cassava are staples. A little peanut sauce is added, as well as a spoonful of cabbage and, sometimes, a bit of beef or chicken. Nyette is a traditional dish made with a kind of sorrel that grows on the banks of the Nile, which meanders across the city.

The most commonly spoken languages in and around the capital are Bari, Juba Arabic and English. A driver tells me he can speak eight languages. He learned them when he was a refugee, like millions of other South Sudanese.

The impact of the civil war is still being felt: for every 1,000 newborn babies, 135 will die before the age of five, the highest rate in the world. One in six mothers dies during childbirth, another record. And, in South Sudan, women of child-bearing age do just that, bear children: many of the women draped in colourful cloth who move gracefully along the dusty roads, unlikely catwalks, are pregnant.

Life goes on and on Saturday nights, drums and chanting can be heard across neighbourhoods. Near our residence, the partying stops in time for the muezzin's call to prayer, just before sunrise. Then the faithful in their Sunday best start singing hymns in the packed Dinka church.

My father loved me. He was also fond of knives.

When he fell ill with cancer, I was able to spend every day of the last three months of his life with him at home, then at the local clinic and, at the end, in the regional hospital.

He developed back pain, from all the sitting. I offered to massage him but he was reluctant. I'm sure he was embarrassed at the thought of his daughter touching him in a way that could be seen as intimate. But when he got mouth ulcers from the chemotherapy, he asked me to rub medicated gel into his gums so he could get some relief. He was also too weak to bite his nails and, for the first time in decades, they needed trimming: Would I please use the penknife he always carried, just in case, in the pocket of his trousers hanging in the wardrobe? My mother scolded him: What? A sick man, bringing a knife into hospital? This must be a first, he would be expelled if it was discovered. She said she had finally had enough of his eccentricities. Two hours later, I peeled the apple the nurse had brought in and I fed it to my father, who ate it with his eyes closed. It was his last meal.

After his death on a rainy Summer's day in July 2011, we shared his belongings. He wanted his youngest son to have his prayer book, his shaver and his camera. That was his only wish. In a cabinet in his study, we found half a dozen knives bound together. He had sworn by the quality of a certain brand and bought a selection for each of his children, the only present he had given us as adults. My siblings had collected theirs years earlier but I lived abroad and since I could not pack mine in my carry-on luggage, they were still waiting for me. I took the penknife out of the bunch. My initials had been carved into the cowhorn handle. I put it into my handbag, just in case.

Three years later, I'm waiting in an office in the National Security building in Jebel, Juba. I have been summoned, without notice this time. One of the three armed men in uniform is practising his shooting skills on a computer with a mouse and I am waiting. And waiting. And I freeze. I remember in a flash my penknife in my handbag. The detector at the entrance failed to pick up the steel blade. It must have been out of order. I no longer dread the talking-to and its consequences (the authorities say they do not "interrogate" journalists, months into the fresh conflict, they just give them "advice"). What if I am asked to empty my bag, as I was requested to do by half a dozen armed men during my first visit a fortnight ago?

The next day, a colleague taking me to the airport asks if there are mango trees in England. I say we have apples and he smiles. It is his favourite fruit, he says: during the war, he survived on fruit and rain water in a forest for six years.

Radio presenters in Juba say good weather is expected when rain is on its way.

About the author:

Gabrielle Papin has worked with words as a journalist and story writer (and, earlier, as a translator/interpreter and language teacher). South Sudan, Ireland and French Polynesia are some of the countries she has lived in which made the strongest impression.

THE SUDAN I KNOW
by Ali Abdulla Ali Ramram

I was a one year old when my family and I moved to the UK from Sudan. My first ever visit to my birth country was 10 years later at the age of 11. A journey which changed my views on the world, that along with the Autobiography of Malcolm X.

London in the early '90s had many young families who moved to the UK from Sudan: some for political reasons; others for economic ones; many were for both. My family and I were very much accustomed to our Sudanese culture and maintained them; nevertheless I had no recollection of my birth place before my first return visit. My older siblings and parents would sometimes mention stories of their years in Sudan and in the midst of it, I heard names of my uncles and aunts in passing.

My Siblings and I went to an Egyptian Saturday School to learn Arabic in North London. The standards at the school were high; we would sit our exams at the Egyptian Embassy and would need to pass the end of year exams in order to progress. The school followed an identical educational curriculum to Egypt and the exam papers would be sent there to be marked. We had a vast amount of homework due to the school being open only once a week yet the content was the same as a student attending school daily in Egypt. There were a good number of us at the school from Sudanese backgrounds. Lunchtime was the most enjoyable time at the school, during which we would play football. My older brother was by far the best player in the school; we would frequently play Sudan Vs Egypt depending on what country we were from. At times, others from Eritrean backgrounds would sometimes join our team, partly because they saw themselves culturally closer to us and partly because we were fewer in number. Although they outnumbered us, we always beat the Egyptians at their own school.

As a youngster we attended many Sudanese weddings in London. I remember Sudanese singers like Mohammed Wardi and Kamal Tarbas at various weddings or concerts as I was growing up. Abdelkarim Al-Kabli even resided at our home for over a month in London during his visit to the UK. My favourite video tape was of Wardi during his concert in Addis Ababa, Ethiopia. I grew up memorising the lyrics to his songs not knowing what they meant. I was impressed by the number of musicians in his band and in particular the saxophone. The discipline they all demonstrated was memorable. He was my favourite musical artist during my childhood. I still recall when I first saw him performing in London live. At the time I believe he was in exile from Sudan and mainly resided in Egypt. I must have been seven or eight when my family and I went to one of his live shows. I remember going to see him backstage after the first half of his live show and told him I was a big fan. After our brief chat I asked for his telephone number, which he kindly scribbled down. I called him the next day and we had a long conversation.

Similarly, I was exposed to Sudanese politics from a young age. My father would frequently take me to Sudanese Political meetings and conferences mostly held by the opposition parties. My father was against the regime but had no allegiance to any particular opposition group; he would attend most political meetings held in London and some were even held at our home. As a child, I would sometimes sit in and listen to what they had to say but to me, they all sounded the same! These men would have a meal, drink three or four cups of tea and have various conversations about how the current government had robbed the country of its resources and how the good old days were much better than the current state. I was disinterested but even so I enjoyed sitting in and listening to elders' conversation.

Two conferences I vividly remember were of Mohammed Osman Almarghani and John Garang – two prominent political party leaders during that period. There was a great buzz and anticipation before they were presented to their respective conferences. I was eleven at the time and remember Almarghani's conference was quite a boring one, he would laugh at his own jokes and I could not understand what the build-up was all about. Garang on the other hand was much more charming. I remember all the guests had to be searched before entering the conference by welcoming security guards. I felt special as a child being searched for the first time to see if I carried a weapon with me on entering the conference. I knew there was a civil war in Sudan but did not know what it was really all about. I could tell by the conference that Garang was really passionate about his cause and that a lot of the crowd members saw him as their champion for their struggles.

Now to my first visit to Sudan. It was December of the year 2000 before I would first return to the country that I had left at the age of one; I was accompanied by my father and my older brother. I had no real expectations but I was excited and my father was the most thrilled. Most of our heavy luggage was presents to family members in Sudan. I knew that both my mother and father were the eldest of their siblings and that they both had big families. As we boarded the plane in London, my father to my embarrassment smoked a cigarette on board inside the small toilet: we could all smell it. This led to the pilot eventually giving him a warning that if he smoked again on the plane, it would be a great risk to passengers and that he would face serious consequences. I was concerned that my father would be asked to leave the plane before take-off but luckily the rest of the journey was uneventful.

We eventually arrived in Sudan around midday greeted by the hot Sudanese Sun as we exited the plane's door. My brother and I were bored at the airport so we exited the main area of the airport whilst my dad was occupied with customs. As we exited, my brother and I saw a group of around thirty people waving at us, I knew it was my family as one person looked almost identical to my father yet looked twenty years older than him. I knew my paternal grandfather had passed away so could not make sense of who this man was. My brother and I were partly excited yet surprised and slightly fearful, we decided to go back to our father near customs rather than greet our relatives alone. I was later to find out that the man who looked like my father was one of his younger brothers of about ten years age difference.

We finally got out of the airport and were welcomed by about eight cars full of family members. For the next few days we would be greeted further by endless family members. I saw tears of joys from women and men alike. It was difficult to understand the endless love at first. My aunts would tell me stories of how they used to hold me when I was only a one year old, before we had left and would constantly grab my chubby eleven year old cheeks and kiss me, particularly my maternal grandmother. They all spoke to me as though we had been together my whole life.

We stayed in Khartoum for another 10 days or so before we made the journey to our hometown Nuri, in the north of Sudan. There was a marked difference between the two places. Khartoum was a busy capital yet basic infrastructure was still poor. Nuri on the other hand had a very different feel to it.

Nuri was surprisingly green and leafy considering it is geographically located in the Sahara desert. The hospitality and the warmth there was to a different level altogether as we were invited nearly every day to someone's home and they would often slaughter a sheep for us and hold a gigantic evening feast. Sometimes they would ask us to pick a sheep from the herd and within a few hours it would be on our plate, barbecued. Talk about fresh meat!

The mangos and palm trees in Nuri's water valleys impressed me and we would stroll in the gardens that belonged to my late grandfather to pick mangos. Nearly every week there would be outdoor parties with a traditional Shaygi singer playing a unique instrument called the Tanbur, I did not understand the lyrics but enjoyed the rhymes and tribal dances in particular.

But there was another side to my trip to Sudan. It was equally memorable: Poverty. In the streets of Khartoum the capital, I saw limbless beggars in the hot Sun begging; sometimes they would knock at the window of the car at a traffic light. Back in London, I was aware that I grew up in a notorious part of the city and possibly one of the most deprived areas in the UK, Peckham. However, the poverty that I witnessed in Khartoum made me appreciate many things I had in the UK. I also saw how highly Sudanese valued education, elders and youngsters alike. I had relatives who were my age that would sometimes study with no electricity due to power cuts, at times it would be hot and little daylight would be available. Yet I saw a determination to succeed in some of them regardless of their sometimes dire circumstances. My subsequent visits to Sudan would become more frequent, either yearly or every 2 years at most. Rediscovering my roots made me appreciate the educational opportunities that I had back in London.

The year I visited Sudan for the first time was also the same year I switched my Saturday school in London from the Egyptian one, previously mentioned, to a Sudanese one. The standard of teaching at my new Sudanese school was very poor for learning Arabic. The teachers at the school would frequently ask me if I had recently moved to the UK from Sudan. They were impressed when I told them I had lived in London since the age of one. I had convinced my parents to stop sending me to the Egyptian School. I told them I wanted to focus on my secondary school studies, but the real reason was because I did not want to continue with their high homework demands. In my new school I was the best in my class, and was quickly promoted to the most senior class, where I was the youngest.

I owed my good Arabic to the Egyptian school I had attended since the age of one and more so to my mother who would spend hours each evening teaching me and my siblings. The best class I enjoyed at the new school and where I felt I learnt something meaningful was the Sudanese history class. I was the most interested student in the class and would ask the teacher engaging questions. I soon stopped attending Arabic classes at the school because the standards were too low, but ironically I only went in to study English. We had a retired English teacher named Rod Usher who had spent two years in Sudan in his early twenties, as a volunteer. He taught English differently to my secondary school teachers and to my surprise he emphasised the importance of the Arabic language, being bilingual and maintaining our Sudanese link more so than the Sudanese teachers at the School. Similarly, Mr Usher would emphasise the importance of the English language. He played a big part in me gaining entrance to study medicine at Cambridge. I would not have gained a place there had I not scored well in my English exams which were largely due to his lessons. I still maintain a very close friendship with him until this day and he invited me to get involved in the Creative Writings from the Sudans project which led to the publishing of this book.

I continued to maintain my bilingualism throughout university and studied Arabic, theology and Islamic history in my third year of my medical studies at Cambridge. I regularly visit Sudan and hope to either live there or be closely associated with it for the rest of my life. I keep an active interests in Sudanese projects and associations that aim to better my beloved country.

About the author:

Ali is a Sudanese born medical doctor who regularly visits the Sudan. His two most inspirational figures in life are his mother Iman and father Abdulla. He maintains strong links with family and friends back home and is involved with different groups which aim to help and promote Sudan and its people.

THE SWEET SMELL OF EXCESS

By Osama Mahmoud Salih

From the air just before dawn breaks
A blaze of lights proudly boasting
Khartoum's expansion, girth, power, wealth
Seeking to emulate that other immoral success story carved out of a desert
Just accept and be humbled by its success
Do not be tempted to examine closer
A diamond encrusted mirage expertly set in a band of water
A Jewel on the Nile
Or perhaps not a jewel on closer inspection
Perhaps the discarded yellow foil of an old sweet
Stamped into the dust yet enough remaining above the surface
Catching the sun, its glint luring the unwary
And fooling them into thinking it gold
Fool's gold

But do not awake just yet
Let the fantasy continue a little longer
Before the dream must end as all dreams must
The sumptuousness of the new million-dollar villas
To house the sumptuous new million-dollar men
And their sumptuous million-dollar trophy wives
At a time where it is more important to be seen to be rich
Than to actually be happy
And where the word rich has suffered the same fate as the currency
Hopelessly devalued
So that it raises not a single eyebrow
That a wedding singer is demanding six million local scraps to sing for an hour
But if you expect his new songs then it will cost you eight
Subject of course to you agreeing to change your wedding date
To fit his schedule
To provide him the opportunity to sing for his supper

And what a supper!
Surely Mighty Rome herself never witnessed such lavishness
An orgy of food, dress, jewels and cars that for a moment dull the senses
Like a cold-war arms race of conspicuous consumption
To maintain your place in society you must outspend your neighbour
Your parties must have more food than his
You must invite more people
They must arrive in better clothes and drenched in more perfume
So as to leave more overstuffed

Just as the world reached a stage where there were more nuclear weapons
Than were needed to destroy it several times over
Then kept on building more

So Khartoum's parties reached a stage
Where more food was provided than was needed to bust the biggest of guts
And kept on catering
You may believe that things have never been better
And for some that is so
Until you glimpse at the fringes of this Utopia
And catch the stench of deprivation hunger and disease only streets away
And stare into the eyes of those who cannot get into these Palaces
Except to seek manual labour
And go home in the evening to their encampments that circle the walls of the new Jericho
And pray for their Joshua
Listen closely and you may think you hear Khartoum fiddle
While Sudan burns

Our Nero's in chariots built in Stuttgart have the tinted windows up and the music loud
Not to be reminded by the common people that they are only emperors of a dung heap
And most of all not to hear the drums of war safely far enough south
Or the cries of the starving far enough west
After all there are still banks that have not been looted sufficiently
And the national coffers can still be squeezed of a few more drops
To add a few more instant millionaires to our lottery economy
Why even the promise of pre-spent oil wealth only spurs ever-greater gluttony
By those smiled upon by fate
Or close enough to power and to the trough
In a rush to build up their cents into dollars
But in no hurry for their dollars to make sense
So our Pompeii continues to fatten happily
Like a sacrificial sheep, not knowing her growing fat is the beginning of her end
Not an end in itself

Or perhaps Khartoum believes herself soaring ever higher like an eagle
But actually being merely a bloated Icarus
Ostentatiously dressed in mock Parisian fashions
Fresh from the sweatshops of Taiwan
With misspelled labels
Emboldened by shameless greed
Intoxicated by ill-gotten wealth
Mollified by false piety
And the sun growing hotter on her temporary wings

About the author:

Osama Mahmoud Salih claims to be a Brit of Sudanese origin. But the truth is probably the reverse. He also claims to be a businessman who writes novels and poetry in his spare time. Again, priorities are in question. That he is a husband and father is not in dispute.

HOME
by Aala Sharfi

Her only company were the crickets. The silence haunted her, so one day she called the young boy next door and she pressed a few notes into his palm. She then asked him to go to the market to buy a clock. The sound of the clock broke the silence and every now and then the loud harmonic *azzan* intertwined with its repetitive ticking. Now it had stopped, as if it had concluded there was no sense in keeping track of the seconds since all her days were the same. She constantly remembered the day they had stood by the door and he had promised her he would come back. Her eyes carried tears while his carried hope, dreams and ambition. Within them she could see how close his dreams appeared to him, as if they were around the corner.

Years later, she now left the veranda door open and the crickets talked her to sleep.

———◦◦◦———

His feet dragged across the ground. He felt heavier than usual today. Perhaps it was the effect of the few hours of sleep he had managed to get last night. Repeatedly startled out of his momentary slumber by the buzzing of excited mosquitos in his ear in the dark. The night sky floated over dreaming Khartoum, its quiet contrasting the energy of the day. The silence was broken only by the sound of his mother's even breathing in the next room. He felt uneasy, uncomfortable. Confusion was the last thing he had expected to feel upon arriving. It had been a few days now but it all hadn't quite sunk in yet. After a few hours of tossing and turning in his bed, he decided to take a walk around the house that was definitely his, yet felt nothing like home. Walking around outside in the middle of the night was not considered safe these days. People had changed. Barefooted, so that he did not disturb her, as if it mattered. His feet adjusted to the cooler tiles with each step and his soles were coated with a light dust that was always present no matter how many hours of the day were spent cleaning.

———◦◦◦———

For months an emptiness filled him and he blamed it on his displacement. The distance away from those he loved and the home he loved had shoveled out his core, leaving him hollow and tired. He spent days ignoring the sunlight coming in through the window of his little room in an attempt to forget about time. He constantly counted the days until he could finally go home; they then turned into months, then years. His broken promise ate at him everyday and he thought maybe if he showed time indifference it would stop teasing him and go about its business faster. With time the guilt got heavier. He thought all that was missing inside him would come rushing back as soon as his feet touched the ground where he was born.

As he made his way down, the warm familiar air filled his nostrils and he inhaled it with an unfeigned desperation to quench his longing thirst. Even though the faces he looked at did not smile back, they soothed him. The tired, worn out bodies that let him through the gates like zombies, looked naively welcoming. This is what he was used to. And as he made his exit out to the blazing sun that blinded his unaccustomed eyes he was bombarded with an atmosphere filled with sweaty embraces and wide smiles, mouthing greetings that were repeated monotonously in an attempt to revive the sincerity lost with their frequency. He felt his happiness overspill and flow around him.

The only word that could describe the look on his face as he gazed out of the window of the crowded bus was awe. He knew he had been away for a while, and the slight transition of the city to incorporate the ill-fitting modernity was understandable. He recognized the roads; some now paved, but the same large Neem trees he once sat under still shaded them. The people that walked the roads all varied in appearance. They could not be described as Africans or Arabs; the country had managed to mother descendants of different backgrounds bringing together hundreds of tribes. Their roots set so deep they all eventually interlaced, endlessly crossing over; here they all belonged; here he belonged.

It was now quieter; traces of the busy city were left behind as he made his way along the spindly alleyways to their front door. He was relieved to see that there had been no changes here, every little stone was exactly where he remembered it. As he stopped by a worn out white door, he paused for a minute in doubt. The geometric bars seemed vaguely familiar but something was wrong, yet as the door swung open he relaxed and recognised the bright blue paint which served as a backdrop to the memory of his last conversation with her; that must have been replaced at some point through the years.

The same beds were neatly arranged around the veranda. Memories of large but intimate gatherings filled with loud conversations and endless laughter rushed back to him, and any excitement that may have settled down on the way home was instantly rekindled. His feet steadily followed the spotless, mismatched tiled path leading to the inside of the house.

Inside lingered the scent of musk, familiarity and attachment. There she was, clothed in embroidered white fabric seated with her back to him. He came to face her and before confusion took over his expression he skillfully concealed it with kind words as he had been taught. He recognised her voice and her posture, but surely he hadn't been away for that long. The frail hands that clutched onto him and the tears that ran down the deep wrinkles spread across her face indicated decades.

<hr />

She had waited for years. Every month she anticipated his letters, crumpled from their journey across the ocean. His words were reassuring: they told her of his success and happiness and of his general content with the way things had turned out. Yet the letters were always filled with excuses, of how he could not come home just yet. Never showing her disappointment, her voice always expressed her joy for him and how much he was missed. She prayed for Allah to bless him and to protect him. She prayed he would come back to her soon.

After the news the house was bustling, sadness choked the air and tears dwelled in every corner. Death had visited before it had taken with it her husband, now her son. It always brought the community together just as well as happiness, however she knew this was the last time it would come.

But now the sympathetic visitors and repeated condolences both sincere and insincere had died down and the house was now emptier than ever. Before the emptiness had a certain lightness, as if it expected to be extinguished by his unexpected arrival; now it was permanent, it had settled in knowing this was the final state. More than often she would imagine him around the house, she would picture his arrival and how he would kiss her forehead, and she would feel his presence around her although she knew it was now too late and it would never happen. Sitting in the now bare veranda, she remembered the past; the chatter of the neighbours and squeals of excited children that could not stay still had been replaced by the sounds of her elderly footsteps dragged around the empty house. The busy social days had now slowed down to silent siestas followed by the usual tea at sunset. Large circular trays of food were now not served in celebration but in traditional routine. The regular unannounced visits that were always welcome; now they were scarce.

<hr>

At first being ignored angered him; he was irritated. Why did people not notice his arrival? The sullen atmosphere around his family home had not changed the least bit since he had been back. He sat in his late father's favourite chair, creases forming on his forehead. His blood boiled but was saved from spilling over by a disappointed sadness. His eyes moved to the wall across from him, it too had changed colour; the cracks he was used to following when he was younger were now all neatly plastered over. A black and white photo of him and one of his father were framed and hung on the wall side by side.

He did not know how long he had been away. He also didn't know how it had taken him so long to find his way back. Parts of his journey had been blocked off and some jumps of memory did not make sense.

The glorious days of his generation were far-gone. The air of Sudanese community and hospitality still floated above the country yet it failed to sink in and fully infuse within its streets. People no longer walked with their heads held high. Their shoulders drooped with the strains a new time had brought. And his shoulders drooped with the realisation of what his time away had stolen from him, and all that he had missed.

Days passed and he began to see how his excitement had previously blinded him. He observed life from afar, taking in all the changes, unnoticed. It seemed as though all the things that defined his home still existed but had somehow lost their spirit. Hawkers paused by cars selling everything from seasonal fruit to coat hangers and mirrors. Dusty children tapped on European car windows with burdens that he sensed were too heavy for their immature shoulders. They ran across the roads as if the cars were their playmates in a game of tag, manoeuvring around the congested labyrinth with innocent hopes of palms offering them solace through a window. He joined a group of men under a tree for their morning tea and coffee. Dust covered his toes and he welcomed it, as it was a sign of his movement around the city, a suggestion of life, it entertained his illusion of existence. He watched everyone move around him, he enjoyed the bustling company even though they were unaware of his presence. The lady served drinks in tiny teacups, mechanically; she wore a sadness that was obvious, contrasted by the bright patterned tobe wrapped around her. Young and old they all bonded over their hardships.

Family had become an obligation rather than a blessing. Weddings were larger and grander than ever. Lights that covered the mansion like homes shone brightly like beacons marking the spot of celebration. Thousands of guests spilled through the doors, donning displays of their deceivingly effortless, untainted wealth. They wore masks of false happiness and eyes wandered with scrutiny. Courtesy had become a lifestyle. People were too concerned with their own difficulties. Yet, it was not selfishness, it was an imbalance of priorities. Despite the time's tribulations, generosity still prevailed, there were no 'individual' misfortunes, difficulties were dealt with as a community. If anything, the city radiated with culture, it was worn with pride. Emphasis was placed on age-old traditions as a desperate attempt to grip   what could so easily be lost in the midst of strong foreign influence. He was comforted by the assurance that values and customs still held their importance, yet he worried for the family. They depended on the faltering youth which was occupied with the same dream of leaving, aiming to find an easier life elsewhere. Regret consumed him: he once shared similar ambitions and now that it was too late he knew that foreign affluence could never replace the unparalleled things his home offered him. He wished he could pass on this newfound wisdom.

Afternoon walks gave him time to reminisce while everyone rested indoors avoiding the heat. He imagined his memories replayed, set within his new surrounding reality; after all, the city had not changed much in appearance. He had grown accustomed to the changes and had accepted that change was inevitable. Despite everything he still had hope that all previous glory would be restored. Fifteen minutes later he started to notice he had been going in circles. He chuckled as he remembered getting lost was normal for him; all the modest brick houses and little sandy roads looked the same. From a distance a man was waving at him, he recognised his neighbour's white smile framed by his dark mahogany skin. He had adapted to his invisibility. Yet he sometimes took pleasure in pretending he was as physical as he felt. It wasn't that he did not sense the blanket of sadness that lay over the inhabitants of the city; it was just that the sadness had become strangely comfortable.

He was home. This was home.

About the author:

Aala Sharfi (20) is an architecture student in the UK. A childhood spent both abroad and in Khartoum, as well as her ongoing university experience are generators of inspiration and ultimately, the realization of the importance of home. For her, Sudan will eternally present a comfort and a sense of belonging that is not found elsewhere.

THE SUDAN AND I
by Gemeela Sherif

The smell of *turaab* wakes me up in the morning,
The damp dust settles under my nose and I arise from my deep
sleep.
I wash under the shower head which calms my breathing and
freshens my skin.
The angry Sudanese sun is already waiting for me outside,
Ready to burn deep into my bones as I move along the tarmac.
My shoes fill with sand and my toes heat as the grains edge their
way into the crevices.
My local shopkeeper *salaams* me, the same bright smile he offers
me every morning, the same joyful tone.
I leave with my bag of oil, sugar and eggs.
I wave my hand to flag down a *rickshaw* as I am too exhausted to
walk,
We agree a price after I haggle and plead that I only have two
pounds left.
I sit and sigh, look around at my town, my people and the world
as I know it;
The faces of innocence which greet me daily,
The hands of need which I fill with spare change,
The donkeys on the roadside wonder looking for shade.
This is Sudan, *my* home, *my* people, *my* county as I know it.

About the author:

I am half Sudanese and half English. I moved to Sudan to teach for over 3 years and became more in touch with my Sudanese culture. I have continued to keep an interest in Sudan, and have started studying Arabic in my free time. I'm very proud of my Sudanese heritage and want others to know more about it.

Illustration by Hussein Merghani

THE CAMEL AND THE NILE
by Yasmin Sinada

In a small flat somewhere in Europe, where she lived with her family, was a brown and white poster stuck to the wall. It had a huge camel and the letters spelling SUDAN on it. For someone only eight years old that huge poster covering half the wall made an impact. This was some faraway African land that this young girl was, and was not part of. In her little head there was some longing, but also a bit of an annoyed feeling going on, as she studied that camel. For this was the reason why she was different. This is where her black father sat, right under that poster, on his bed, and cried for the first time when they got the news that her grandfather had died. He died somewhere far away, on the other side of that poster.

———◦———

30 years later…

It was so hot, and Laila just sat there day-dreaming. The sweat was running down the tunnel of her back and around her waist – a wet belt formed. She took a deep breath and the smell of the lime tree she sat under overwhelmed her. Different scents always transferred her somewhere else in time and place. It was always somewhere where she felt protected and completely serene and into what one would call happy childhood memories. You could even say the smell of limes was a good thing. She remembered her grandmother. As long as her grandmother was alive, this place, this world was safe. She covered Laila in her magical prayers, with her secret verses, as grandmother for sure had a link to God that very few had. This made her feel warm. She took a deep breath and sighed, "If only haboba Nazli was here today". These days the anxiety creeps in, the teeth clench, the body stiffens as Laila battles the daily comings and goings. Over there towards the West, where she now lives, there is no magic to protect her, no strength of pride to hold her up. But it is mainly the magic, the magic that is missing. And life without it is just plain hard. Especially now that Laila was made vulnerable by this great treasure she has been given to keep safe. Ever since she has laid her eyes on her children, got so unimaginably attached, and felt the enormity of responsibility for them, so has she also become constantly alarmed.

If only she had the magic to calm her down, to untie the knots, to un-clench the teeth, to feel at ease… , "Where are you haboba Nazli"? "May God almighty forgive your sins and put you up in Fardose, the Highest of Heavens…Yes, I know, you are here, you are in my prayers." Laila sighs.

———◦———

Time to get in the car and go for a drive. They pass the river. Laila wants the driver to stop, she wants to look at it, touch it, breathe it. This river, the Nile, is alive, as it has been for thousands of years. She feels its power, its beauty, its strength and length. The driver does not stop, there is no time, there are things to be done, there are people to please, there is stress in living the moment. Laila just wants the car to stop, she wills the car to stop, she hopes the car will stop, she knows it will not…, and for a millisecond a thought runs through her mind, a reoccurring thought of next time, but there will be no next time, this moment will not be there again… this moment. The Nile, the Mother of all rivers, forever pregnant, eternal… But not everyone notices the magic, they don't feel the time in the river, they don't hear the knowledge it carries, how much it has seen, how much Laila wants to be part of it and connect with it. For this girl is also timeless somehow, disconnected from the present, but very much connected to some other meaning that not everyone can see. The beauty of nature, the beauty inside all the people who have crossed her path, the oneness of it all and somehow this place, the Sudan, the Nile the center of it all. She feels great pride in being Sudanese, in the rich culture, in the beautiful people she is part of, from being from the Nile, for understanding the mystical language of 'alif' and 'ba'. For the heat of the sun, for the sound of the Azan, grateful for being able to visit and smell the lime tree and be close to the magic of this desert land and her ancestors. Yes, she has finally crawled inside the poster and embraced him.

———— ⟨∞⟩ ————

The feeling of being out of control starts creeping in and hurting her pride, the mind wonders…but wasn't my grandfather a Sheikh and my great grandfather a Faki, the magic is there from both sides, she feels the strength, she feels the connection, she feels the river, she smells the river, she is one with it, no need to stop the car, no need to see the Nile, no need to stand by it. She is living the past and the future and the present for a moment there…

Time to board the plane, lift it up with prayers, land it down with prayers and clench those teeth and fight the routine of the days through meditation, to pass the test, to keep the balance and to direct those little ones on the right path, to support their strengths, to fight their weaknesses, to nurture their faith, to make them compassionate, to restrain their selfish, and their angry, to make them connect with the Nile even through the distance, to remind them of their land and who they are, and to build up their pride even if they are so different. For all those moments, all those scents and all those feelings are here now; for the present, the future, and the past are all here through magic and prayer.

About the author:

My mother is Czech and father Sudanese. I spent my childhood in Prague, Aden, Khartoum and later on, in London. I did my postgraduate studies in England and worked as an IT consultant. Currently, home is Germany with my Sudanese husband and two sons who are my full time occupation.

THE BAOBAB TREE
by Yasmin Sinada

A monkey from the forest leapt into their garden, landed;
On top of the Baobab Tree

'*Sit al shai*, selling tea, smiley face, keeping cool;
in the shade of the Baobab Tree

A handsome couple, eye to eye, longing so;
Hidden in the shadow of
the Baobab Tree

Above the head in the sky, steaming hot, blazing down;
On the crown

Between the Niles, Blue and White, Tuti Island, green and calm;
Stands alone

Where Tuti ends and they meet, at the Mogren, grows roots deep;

Omdurman, Dervish men, twirling round,
dreads are long, heads are high;
Across the yard

Children running for some gum,
make a stop at Hamad's shop,
On the corner

Funeral tent, stretching out, on the road from the house;
Smiling down

Wedding chants, red and gold, henna hands, 'zaghroots' long;
Dancing is the Baobab

Old man, turban white, slow in pace, 'H' tattooed on his face, strolling by;

'*Tobed*' lady, wrinkly faced, making perfume with crocodile nails;
smelling divine

Famous Gisma with her drums, back up girls and frantic fun,
'*jirtik*' party, wedding dance;
Shaking is, and in a trance;

Wedding night on a stage, long black hair, beautiful face,
Outstretched arms and outstretched legs,
The rest of her soft and shakes,
Groom is swaying, feeling dizzy,
No more free, is the Baobab Tree

Late at night or afternoon,
All the women meeting soon,
Drums are beating, dancing frenzy
Dressed in RED, they are plenty
This is 'Zaar', the counseling sessions
For the ladies releasing tensions.
Recording stories on its knee
Is, The Baobab Tree

Donkey carts on the street
Selling carrots, pepper and beat,
Crossed legged, 'markoub' feet
Is the farmer, feeling heat
Next stop, the Baobab Trees

Fish market and 'basta' sweets,
Morada is full of treats,
'souq' Khartoum is where you go
get your spices when they're low,
by the Nile in Bahri town
Baobab is feeling down.

Haboba's house and crispy sheets
'Anghareb' and 'bambar' seats
Furniture from rope and wood
'bakhoor,' is the sandal wood
Lifted up, in esprit,
are the old Baobab Trees

Tamarhind and Gungulez
Foul soudaani and Aradeb
Mullah rob, Dom and Loz
Kisra, Shata, Balah and Moz
Karkade and Lemon Tee
Thirsty is the Baobab Tree

In Nyala , Kordofan
Dongola and Port Sudan

They all know the Baobab

They are Sudan,
They are the crown,
They are the branches and the roots
Of the Baobab.

About the author:

My mother is Czech and father Sudanese. I spent my childhood in Prague, Aden, Khartoum and later on, in London. I did my postgraduate studies in England and worked as an IT consultant. Currently, home is Germany with my Sudanese husband and two sons who are my full time occupation.

THE OLD MAN OF GEZIRA
by Piran Treen

Morning and the minarets moan.
The earth reverberates
with the banks of the river yawning.

He rises,
broken pyramid abrupt,
from the sand in his sheets.
The old man of Gezira shivers when the sun's up.
After his ablutions he spends the day
cutting the grass with his beard.

In the souq he rattles his teeth at the tea lady,
three guineas for jebana really is too much.
His rage burns hotter than the embers
in her tin can stove.

At *fatur* the teachers moan,
"every day *fuul*",
then wait in line as the *shai* is passed.

The sun is in its zenith
and the world chants in its turning.
He sleeps under an acacia,
a lamb and a goat kid tucked into the folds of his *jalabiya*.
He dreams of the time he travelled from Port Sudan to Kassala:
of the men who melted like dust breaths from the dunes
and sat in the gangway their swords rested across their crossed legs.

He feeds his goats dried sugar cane
and adds salt to their water.
He mashes dates with their milk for his wife.
She sweeps the Sahara from the yard daily.

In the afternoon the crickets are buzzing.
He planted limes and guavas in his garden.
Around them he hollowed squares in the earth,
to hold in the water.

The heat is like water then,
it drowns the land.

Punctuality and anger become foreign things,
reserved for countries where it is too cold
to stay exposed.

They say a big chair does not make a king.
But, Ya Syed, may your imma be wrapped many times around,
may it never come loose in your wanderings,
may you wave your stick with vigour at the wedding singers,
that they may know you are a great man.

Dusk falls and the moon stretches
and plays its oud
as the sky puts on her dark bespangled *tobe*.

He lies under the guava trees
and breathes in their greenery.
His dreaming in the gloam
chugs like a barge across the Nile.
He grumbles about guava eaters.

In his poverty he refreshed his guests
with home made scents.
In his wealth he fed them with the meat
of four strong sheep.

The dervishes gather
as the donkeys braying mixes with the night exhaling.
They sing their songs to the sky
and will chant until the morning.

He will sleep with his doors unlocked,
upon a woven-string bed,
his thoughts taken away by the night
like the riders of a camel train.
When the wind blows his footprints away,
they will surround him with a conical dome.
And all the people of Al Hilaliya will come.
The earth will reverberate
"There lies a man of Gezira".

About the author:

Piran Treen is an amateur writer who came to know Sudan as a conversational English volunteer teacher in Gezira and Kassala, Sudan.

Illustration by Mutaz Mohamed

First Steps into Africa
By Rod Usher

Introduction:

Dr Tony Husband and his wife Wendy were well-established British professionals in El Obeid when I arrived in 1963. Tony was the principal surgeon and medical director of Kordofan; Wendy had been the Matron of the El Obeid Civil Hospital.

Although Wendy and Tony have been dead many years now I decided to send them a letter describing what it was like for me as a very young person stepping on Sudanese sand for the first time.

Dear Wendy,

When I met you and Tony in the early part of 1964 I realised how much you had both loved the Sudan and its peoples. Both of you had worked in the Sudan Medical Service in various parts of the country and had eventually made El Obeid your home. Being invited to your beautiful house, with wild animals wandering around in the garden and inviting themselves into 'conversations' was, for me, an extraordinary experience.

As time went by I was able to take the school bus from Khor Taggat and visit you on a Friday. Both you and Tony offered your friendship to me, and helped me to know more about various parts of Sudan in which you had worked - separately and together. I remember how you both arrived in Sudan: Tony hopped across the border from Ethiopia at the end of the Second World War, and you arrived from London to work as a Nursing Sister in the early 1950s. Medical services in Sudan were developing fast and you were both admired for the contributions you made away from the central focus, in those years, of Khartoum and Omdurman.

When I arrived in 1963 primary and intermediate schools were already strong - but secondary schools were few, and very selective; only a small proportion of successful students went on to a secondary school. I was fortunate to be sent by the government to a large, thriving boarding school which already had a fine reputation. Wendy, you had trained at Addenbrooks Hospital in Cambridge and took the brave step to apply to the Sudan Medical Service, and learn Arabic before you started work; Tony learned his Arabic as part of his daily routine. Earlier he had been in Ethiopia for several years as one of only two doctors within the Friends Ambulance Unit - a pacifist Quaker organisation which offered medical services within war zones, without participating in combat. Both of you were experienced, effective and holding key positions by the time I arrived in Khartoum. Tony was a qualified doctor before he went to Ethiopia; now he was an experienced surgeon.

You told me, Wendy, how you flew out from London in a Varsity aircraft - not very comfortable and certainly slow by later standards. You stopped first in southern France, then Malta, next in Cairo and again at Wadi Halfa before landing in Khartoum. It took several days. How different it was for me, in 1963: propellors had been replaced by jet engines; a flight which took you days took me only a few hours But even more extraordinary was how you travelled on to your first posting in Malakal: you went by flying boat - taking off on the Nile and landing on the Nile, hundreds of miles to the south. You flew over an untouched landscape with small villages as the only markers, once you were south of Kosti. What an experience.

Would you be interested in my own departure to post colonial Sudan, only 15 years after you? By the early 60s Africa was opening up; the 'wind of change' was starting to blow through the continent; many young British people were eager to have experience in this new world, away from colonial attitudes. We wanted to work alongside local people and share experiences with them, rather than bring ready-made solutions from alien cultures.

Towards the end of my second year at university reading Geography, I decided to apply to serve with Voluntary Service Overseas; a few friends in my year were also applying - it was thought to be a valuable experience once those three wonderful university years were concluded. During Finals year I was called to interview in London and was selected as someone suitable to serve overseas for a year, in a capacity to be decided by the host country.

At that time a large number of young graduates were flying off to various corners of the world to serve, mainly as teachers but also as vets, community workers, nurses and a variety of other roles, depending on their qualifications. 1963 was the first year that volunteers had to be qualified by either degree or professional training. As the end of the summer term approached friends announced where they were to go once they left Nottingham: India, West and East Africa, South America, and some travelling to the Pacific Islands. My official papers suggested I was one of the first to be offered a place with VSO and yet no placement arrived, and the weeks dragged on. Why was I to be left out? Meanwhile, you and Tony were working in El Obeid

My Professor, fully supporting my desire to go and work overseas, agreed to call the British Council and enquire about my prospects. He was told that there had been a delay but I had been singled out to be the first ever volunteer to go to Sudan, once the government in Khartoum agreed to the principle of accepting well-intentioned young people to work alongside local professionals. Clearly there was an on-going debate about this break with tradition in Khartoum and this had delayed a final decision. Prior to this, expatriate teachers from Britain and Egypt had been recruited and given formal contracts as teachers. The idea of allowing volunteers into the country was a departure from normal practice in newly independent Sudan.

How much did you know about Sudan when you arrived as a Nursing Sister, Wendy? Sadly my university studies had not informed me on the Sudan! It was easy to read of grizzly historical episodes, which did not fit my idea of service in the developing world. In fact, I was dismayed to find how little was said or even known about Sudan, apart from it being a vast country - the largest in Africa - which straddled cultural, linguistic, religious and ethnic boundaries. Sudan is, it seemed, at the major crossroads in north-east Africa. I also found that there was little infrastructure - apart from a few railways lines, almost certainly built to transport troops as well as goods in the long period when Sudan was governed as a condominium by Egypt and Britain. There were virtually no roads, only a tiny number of airstrips, apart from the International Airport of Khartoum, and few ways of travelling from one part of the vast country to another. It sounded very exciting. Would I be allowed to be the first volunteer to work in Sudan?

I had a great deal of enthusiasm and energy but no real experience of teaching or anything else! You and Tony were fully qualified professionals!

At interview - by a distinguished panel of professional London-based elderly people - I was quizzed hard about my motives. I explained I wanted to be a different type of person going out from Britain, without the trappings of colonial ambitions. Several members of the committee were taken aback. When pressed I explained that I was not intending to go anywhere with the Union Jack sewn on my back. There was a shocked look on the faces of many panel members. "But surely Mr Usher you would not go with it under your feet" was the reply. Had I ruined my chances of being selected? Another question asked what I would do if I was teaching in an African country and went to school one day only to find that the students were on strike. I explained that this was a most unlikely scenario, and anticipated moving to the next question. I was pressed: but what would I do? Again I tried to make light of the question, but was once again pressed to give an opinion. To the Chairman I explained that if I did find this situation I would write and tell him how I had responded! Two weeks after starting work at Khor Taggat Secondary School in El Obeid the whole school went on strike: I wrote a long and detailed letter to Mr Bunting, formerly of the British Council, and explained what I did, and much more besides. That started a helpful and prolonged correspondence with someone who understood the world into which I had recently travelled

The Government in Khartoum agreed to accepting two VSOs that September, and I was to be one of them. Adrian, the other volunteer, was sent to Rumbek Secondary School which closed 3 weeks after he arrived because of civil strife in the area - and it did not open again for many years. Poor Adrian was then bitten by a rabid dog, suffered the agony of immediate treatment in Rumbek and was then repatriated to Britain. I was then the only volunteer in Sudan until the first female VSO, Hope Bury, arrived in August 1964, to teach English at El Obeid Girls Secondary School. You will remember, Wendy, what a lovely fresh Scottish Lass Hope proved to be. We are both now retired, of course, but I see her from time to time in her beautiful Scottish home.

By mid-August 1963 I was to spend two weeks at Goldsmith's College in London for 'orientation'. While many of the several hundred volunteers were sharing sessions with those who had first hand experience of the countries to which they were being sent, there was nobody present who had been to Sudan! In fact Adrian and I were briefed by a junior member of the British Council, who furnished us with papers normally given to those who were destined to work either at the British Embassy or the British Council. At mealtimes, I heard the adventures which lay ahead for those who were going to well-established posts in many countries, generally with close links to Britain. One piece of information which was pressed upon me was that "British people do not use public transport". Within weeks I could have asked, which public transport?

How I wish I could have spoken to you, Wendy, about the life that lay ahead for me: the climate; the problems of communicating with home in England; the joy and friendship of Sudanese hospitality. I left for Africa knowing so little, After 2 years at Khor Taggat I returned to Britain brim full of experiences, enthusiasms for Sudan, and with friendships which have endured to this day.

Amazingly, my Sudanese visa stated I was a Senior Government Official. Nothing could have been further from the truth: I was a smiling young man who had arrived to teach but, in fact, was about to learn.

August 29th, 1963 was departure day. I was given a return ticket to Khartoum, via British Airways. I took off from Heathrow aboard a Comet 4 of Central African Airways - bound for Salisbury and Lusaka. I had flown once before - in a very old Dakota to channel hop on geography field work to France. Now I was lifting off at a very steep angle in the first ever jet passenger airliner. All passengers were white - there was not a black face on board. After a short stop in Rome we flew out through the night and were over Egypt as dawn rose over the desert. This was Africa! Soon we were losing height to land in Khartoum at dawn. In those early years of jet travel international flights came in and out avoiding the heat of the day. The cabin door was opened and the blast of hot air surrounded me: it was 6 am. It would get warmer. How different all this was to your first slow flight, Wendy until you landed by the side of the Nile. Tony had merely driven across the border from Ethiopia.

I was met by university staff (from my home town in England) and by the Inspector for English teaching in Sudan - Stanley Hall. First to the Grand Hotel for a sleep after the long flight from London. By 1pm I was up and about and opened the balcony door of my darkened hotel room: by now the heat was fierce in the sun. Was I to live and work in this sort of heat? How?

A tour of Khartoum and then, more importantly for my African orientation, Omdurman. This eye-opening drive was followed by a meeting at the British Council. Still no notion of where I was to go - clearly I was not going to live in the Grand Hotel, even though the cost was the princely sum of £5 per night. I still had not met a single Sudanese person: the British were keeping me for themselves.

Two days later I was driven to the Ministry of Education; at last I met Sudanese administrators. After discussions - and limoon - papers were signed and I was told I would go to a large boys boarding school in Kordofan: Khor Taggat where I was to teach English Language and Literature. What about my geography? It later became apparent that geography was to be taught by Sudanese graduates; English by the British.

After another two days I was driven to the airport to catch the equally old Sudan Airways Dakota flight to El Obeid. Forget Comets and pressurised air travel - this was real; we landed on a grass and gravel strip on the outskirts of El Obeid. A school lorry collected me and drove over the sand and gravel, bouncing into and out of khors, left by short-lived violent rain storms. The 6 mile drive out of town ended at the impressive school estate. Here were boarding houses, dining halls, classrooms, vast brown playing fields and staff houses. Here was the community in which I was to work for two years, amongst impressive students, excellent Sudanese colleagues and a handful of teachers from other countries - including our Welsh Head of English.

The journey from London had been exhilarating, the time in Khartoum had been fascinating but nothing could prepare me for the excitement of arriving at the school and seeing the eager faces of the boys I was going to live amongst.

It must have been the same for you Wendy - that first day after landing on the Nile in Malakal. At least you had the rudiments of Arabic and willing hands to help you in the hospital. For me it was a new landscape, a fascinating new language and a range of colleagues from different backgrounds. You, Wendy were part of a colonial legacy: I was a volunteer arriving into post-colonial Africa. In the 1960s we young volunteers thought we would change the world for ever, and certainly change the way local people thought of the British. Did that happen?

Could I really set these hard-working boys on the same educational path I had recently travelled? The reality was that I was to start my own education in earnest. Certainly I learned more than I taught. The Sudan was about to teach me genuine hospitality. Perhaps most importantly friendships were to be forged which would endure the fast-changing lives of the boys themselves and the life I was to lead back in England.

In 1625 Francis Bacon wrote: "Travel in the younger sort is a part of education; in the elder, a part of experience. He that travelleth into a country before he hath some entrance into the language, goeth to school, and not to travel."

My education had begun.

Although you died in 2005, aged 83, my admiration for you and your life in Sudan is undimmed. I replay our shared love of Sudan and her peoples on a regular basis.

Rod

About the author:

The Sudan chose me: I was sent to work at Khor Taggat School in 1963. My association with Sudan has lasted 51 years already. A very full career in London's education service followed. In retirement I have helped young Sudanese in London with their English studies. A part of me has remained in Africa.

MID-AFTERNOON SUN
by Katie Vosmek

Tuesday 20th April 2004

The mid afternoon sun is strong. A couple of ladies walked out of the building and head towards some tables in the shade. Elham and Hiad are sitting on low chairs next to Manal's stall. She sets up her makeshift tea stall under the arcade every day. Manal is busy washing-up two glasses that were left on the box. Elham and Hiad have just ordered two cups of *karkade*. The silver kettle on the stove is full of water. There is no rush.

Elham is looking for something in her handbag. She is smiling and nodding. She still wears a ring on her middle finger even though she is not married anymore. Her husband divorced her a year and half ago. Elham comes from a well off family and grew up in Qatar. When they all returned to Sudan she got married to a man her family found for her. He was Sudanese, good looking and Elham soon fell in love with him. They had a nice life, very comfortable. It was a happy marriage for about three years until her husband announced that he wanted to marry another woman. The reason was that Elham didn't give him a son. Elham couldn't have children and a second wife would be able to give him what he wanted. As Elham came from a more liberal background she could not come to terms with a traditional Sudanese marriage arrangement. She could not imagine sharing her husband with another woman and asked her husband for a divorce. He agreed. She still loves him but is hopeful that there is another man for her.

The water has boiled and Manal is pouring some into a smaller kettle with dried hibiscus flowers. *Karkade* is best when it is left to brew for some time. Manal is leaving it on the hob for a bit longer. She has got two small glasses ready on a large aluminium tray. A figure appears behind a bougainvillea bush. It's Saida. She is wearing a long blue *niqab* and a veil that covers her face. There is only a tiny opening for her eyes. She comes closer and then greets her two friends and the tea lady. Manal fetches her a plastic chair to sit on.

Saida is wearing a pair of long black gloves to cover her hands. She is still getting used to it. She never used to cover her whole body until recently. She got married nine months ago. Again. Her first husband left for Libya five years after their wedding. They had two beautiful daughters and she pretty much brought them up on her own. They would occasionally hear from their father when they were little but the phone calls got scarcer and scarcer. The last time they heard his voice was a year ago when Saida decided to contact him after ten years of no news. She wanted to ask for a divorce. Her neighbour, a very kind man, offered that he would take her as his second wife. It became clear that her husband was never going to return to Sudan as he was apparently living with another woman in Libya. And he agreed to divorce her. Saida took her time to make a decision about her second marriage. Both of her daughters were grown up and would soon leave the house. She would stay on her own and as much as she found it strange to start a relationship with a neighbour she didn't want to end up old and alone. She married a man she knew for so many years, who lived across the street with his first wife and children. Now they are all one family and she has to respect his wishes. He knows that Saida is an independent and outgoing woman but he doesn't like it anymore. Saida is forbidden to talk to any men, she has to cover her face and obey her new husband but she doesn't mind. She knows she is going to be well looked after.

The newcomer has ordered some cinnamon tea. The tea lady is filling a sieve with a heap of loose tea. She is pouring water over the third cup. The tea is very strong. It's very refreshing in this heat. It's late April and the scorching temperatures are well in mid 40s. Manal is taking a teaspoon out and opening one of the plastic jars that are laid out on top of her little table. She is putting some powdered milk to the tea and stirring it slowly. Saida is talking really loudly; she is chatty as usual. Elham and Hiad are laughing at her joke. Manal is adding a spoonful of sugar to each glass. The drinks are ready and she is placing them on a small metal table in the middle of the ladies.

Hiad is sipping a glass of *karkade*. It matches the colour of her thobe. Her hair is barely covered and the scarf very often slips down her head. She is careless but not carefree. She has something on her mind. Seven years ago her fiancé was sent to fight in the war in Eritrea. He was going to come back and they were going to get married. She was going to wait for him. She started her university studies, graduated, started her second degree and waited. All this time she had no contact with him. Not a single letter. She hasn't stopped thinking about her fiancé but slowly gave up on seeing him again. All her family thought that he simply must have lost his life in the war and she started believing it as well. After six and half years she got engaged to a new man. The wedding is now planned, she is excited. All of a sudden her old love returns from the war. He comes back a different person, exhausted, changed, damaged. Hiad is happy to see him but is now confused. Is it the same person she knew a long time ago? She should have feelings for him but there is also her new fiancé. Does she go through with the wedding and let her old love deal with his own difficulties? Does she cancel her wedding and give a chance to a relationship to develop again between her and her old sweetheart?

Manal is collecting glasses from another table. They go in a bucket full of greyish water. Manal and the three friends are exchanging a few words. They are enjoying their drinks and each other's company. The shade moves and the ladies are exposed to the sun. It's the breeze that makes the mid afternoon heat bearable here in Omdurman.

About the author:

I came to Sudan in 2004 as a volunteer with SVP to teach at the University of Khartoum. During my stay I have come to know some of the strongest, kindest and disarmingly honest people I have ever met. To me there is no other place like Sudan.

Mary's Story
by Zorina Walsh

Salaam,

My name is Mary, I am about 19 years old and I am from the Bari tribe. I live in a small village about 40 km from Juba, the capital of South Sudan. For about 2 years I have had a dreadful condition that affects many of us young girls and younger women who have been given in marriage at a very early age and then become pregnant. It was around 3 years ago that I got married and very quickly became pregnant for the first time. I was quite thin and not very well developed and had extreme difficulty carrying my baby. At the time of the birth I was very scared because it was very painful and the baby just didn't seem to want to come out. I went to the traditional birth attendant who did her best to look after me but my baby was born dead. It was a little girl. I was very unwell and soon afterwards starting passing water and solid bits from my front passage. I know now that I should have gone to hospital, as the birth lady didn't know how to help me. She had helped so many women give birth in the village I thought she knew what she was doing. I wept and wept, as not only had I lost my baby, I was an outcaste because of my dreadful condition. Because of the leaking I smelled terrible and nobody except my brother would help me. My husband would have nothing to do with me.

In November 2010 I heard about some people from England who were coming to do some surgery for people with my sort of condition. There is a big charity called The United Nations Population Fund and they had broadcast on the radio and sent messages about this visit to areas far and wide, and this would be taking place in Juba Teaching Hospital. I talked to my brother about whether I should go and see if I could get help and he said he would take me on the bus to Juba. The roads in South Sudan are terrible and almost non-existent so this was a very difficult journey for me.

When I arrived I met Dr Fiona and Zorina from the small charity that was undertaking these operations. Fiona examined me, as she would be putting a needle in the bottom of my back to make the lower half of my body numb. This would enable the team of surgeons to undertake the surgery and I wouldn't feel any pain. A local doctor was present also so that he could help with the translation, as I only know one or two words of English. Then Dr Tim, one of the surgeons came to see me. He explained that he would be dealing with the surgery needed to stop the solid bits leaking, and another surgeon was coming in 2 or 3 days who would stop the water from leaking. They would be doing the surgery together. Through Dr Dario they explained to me what was going to happen and what to expect afterwards. I think I understood most of it but I was very scared.

The hospital had arranged for a ward to be available for any of us that were having this surgery. On the ward I met Sharon who was the nurse with the team. She welcomed me and gave me a bed, but I had only just settled down when one of the local nurses said I couldn't stay there because it was where they took their rest! I was very upset and cried a lot. Sharon was very kind and took me to another ward and found me a bed but I felt very lonely as nobody else was having the same operation and they ignored me. However, the next day Sharon had been able to get another bed squeezed into the tiny ward and had also managed to get some mosquito nets put up. We could hardly move between the beds we were altogether and supporting each other. Although we were from different tribes we all got along very well. Most of the other patients were quite young but some were older and one had just given birth and had the baby with her. Luckily, her husband was very supportive and came each day. I made friends with Elizabeth who was a bit younger than me but she was lovely and always smiling even though she was desperate like me.

The big charity very kindly supplied food and water each day. Otherwise we would have been dependent upon our families bringing food in and some of us didn't have that luxury. My brother had to return to the village as he was working but promised to come when he could.

The other 2 surgeons then came to see me – Dr Mike and Dr John. They explained the bit of the operation that they were going to do, interpreted through one of the local doctors. It all seemed so frightening but what could I lose? I had to trust somebody if I were to get my life back. Finally the day came when it was my turn for surgery. I walked up to the operating theatre with Sharon and Zorina who were so kind and tried to make me feel less nervous, but I was very frightened and my stomach was churning. When I got to the operating theatre Fiona was there to look after me with the anaesthetic. She put a needle into my back so that I wouldn't feel anything in the bottom half of my body and I felt more relaxed. Then all the surgeons came in, including Dr Dario who was from Juba. I was happy because I knew he would be there to look after me once the others had gone back home; he could speak my language.

The operation took a long time. I am told it was over 6 hours. When I came round I was on a bed just outside the operating theatre and all the surgeons were there. Dr Dario explained what they had done for me. I had a bag on my tummy as bits of the bowel needed to heal before they could do another operation to take the bag away. I was very worried in case they couldn't do that. I rested there for some time before I was taken down to the main ward. Unfortunately, because of the big surgery that I had undergone I could not go back to the ward with the others. Again, I felt so lonely and missed Elizabeth and the others but Sharon and Zorina visited me frequently and bought me water and medicines. I don't know what I would have done without them. It was just as well they did as one of the nurses on the ward shared my medicines with other patients, and when my drip finished it was taken down and I had become very thirsty.

The time came when the team from England had to return home. I remember it well as they all came to see me and gave me lots of bottles of water, fruit and even some of their own money so that I could at least buy the medicines and water I needed. I cried so much – I am not sure whether it was because of their kindness or sadness at seeing them go – probably both.

I had to stay in hospital for several weeks, as I was unable to travel back to my village and then to return for further surgery to remove the bag. Dr Dario undertook this surgery for me and was so kind and gentle. My brother visited me and was able to give me food and water and after a further 2 weeks I was able to go back on the bus to my village. It was again a very rough journey back but I was welcomed into the village and now my life begins again. My husband has another wife but he treats me well enough now. Sadly, I don't think I will ever be able to have children but at least I don't smell disgusting, I no longer feel ashamed and I can now smile again. I thank God for those lovely people from England who have given me my life back. Zorina told me they were from a hospital in England called St Mary's Hospital and they lived on a small island called the Isle of Wight. I can only dream about living on a small island. It sounds so beautiful.

Thank you and God Bless you all.

About the author:

Zorina Walsh is a retired Medical Education Manager who has been closely involved with the St Mary's Hospital, Isle of Wight link with Juba Teaching Hospital, arranging funding, organising training visits (including the vesico-vagina fistula visit in 2010), and has spent a total of nearly 6 months in Juba.

PETER WIGGINS MEETS EMMANUEL JAL, THE SUDANESE HIP-HOP STAR.

By Peter Wiggins

"I am still a soldier. But now my weapon is music."

Emmanuel Jal was a child when the second phase of the Sudanese civil war began. He watched his life collapse before his eyes. His village was burnt down, his aunt was raped, his mother was killed. When he asked who was responsible, people told him that it was the Northern Sudanese. Jal became one of thousands of children who migrated to Ethiopia to live in a refugee camp. At the age of just seven, lusting for revenge, he joined the Sudan Peoples' Liberation Army (SPLA). His aim was to kill Muslims and Arabs.

In 1991 the SPLA, previously united in enmity towards the North, divided along tribal lines. A new civil war emerged between the two biggest ethnic groups in South Sudan, the Nuer and the Dinka. Jal migrated to Juba where he joined the Nuer faction. He then escaped from the war to a town called Waat. It was the wife of Jal's guerrilla commander, a British aid worker called Emma McCune, who saved his life. Insisting that he was too young to be a soldier, she smuggled him to Kenya in the baggage area of a plane.

A few months later Emma was killed in a car crash in Nairobi, Jal sank into a deep depression. Recovering slowly with the help of Emma's friends, he realised that music offered him the hope of a new life. Rapping and writing music, he soon became a rising star in the Kenyan music scene. His first single All We need is Jesus was played endlessly on Kenyan radio. By 2005 Jal was a global star. The Guardian newspaper described him as the 'hottest thing to hit the African music scene for quite some time".

I went to meet Jal at a pub near his home in Finsbury Park. He didn't want a drink. Jal fasts until 5PM each day to raise money for the building of a school in South Sudan. He is not more than a musician. He is a full-time activist.

"Music is powerful", he tells me. "I am still a soldier. But now my weapon is music". I ask him what he is fighting for. "Rights', he declares. "Human beings have rights". Jal is light-hearted, full of jokes and laughter – but with a profound mission in life. Over and above recording his new album, he is also setting up a record label for young unrecognised artists. And then there is his own charity 'Gua Africa' for the rehabilitation and education of former-child soldiers. He is a spokesman for Amnesty International, for the Coalition to Stop the Use of Child Soldiers, and for the Make Poverty History Campaign. "I am really busy", he explains.

Jal's music and his activism go together. When he talks politics, his words still have a poetic feel to them. He speaks with a rhythm of his own. "All my work connects", he explains. Jal takes what he needs from the music that surrounds him. He uses rap and spoken word against a backdrop of African beats. Jal's first album Gua was recorded in English, Arabic, Nuer, Dinka, and Kashwali. The multiplicity of languages was a deliberate plea for understanding. In the same spirit, Jal released an album Ceasefire, alongside a famous Northern Sudanese singer, Abdel Gadir Salim. He laments the glamorisation of violence that has become prevalent in safe Western hip-hop, knowing first hand what violence looks like.

I ask about the relationship between Jal's troubled past and his present. I quote to him the words of Arthur Miller: "we move through the world carrying the past". Jal agrees:

"that's right, you see my past is what inspires me to carry on doing what I do every day. I am doing it for the people whose voices are not being heard. I am doing it for my dreams, for the voices that speak to me, for the dead bodies."

Jal still suffers from nightmares. His most recent single is entitled 'War Child'. Under the same title, Jal has published an autobiography. There is also a documentary film chronicling Emmanuel's early life.

Talking of the troubles of Jals's motherland, we come to his contentment in his new home, London. I am interested to hear him say that it was only in coming to London that he managed to like himself: "Even when I was in Kenya, I hated myself for being a black person". After living in London for four years, he loves the range of place, people and culture. "Everyone here is so friendly to me", he says with a smile.

The politics of identity has been a factor in wars all across Sudan. Jal knows this as well as anyone. "I am Sudanese and I am African", he asserts.

"It is tribalism that has destroyed my country. I am also a Christian but it is not something that I brag about".

It surprises me when he tells me that the North Sudanese are his biggest fans. Every bit of the hostility that Jal once felt towards Muslims has been lost.

"I work with people from the North. There are so many Muslims who are wonderful people." We come to British politics. "Your political system is amazing", he says plainly. I ask him what he thinks about the MPs' expenses fiasco. "Your politicians get into trouble if they steal one pound. You should go to Africa. They steal millions". He laughs loudly. "Your politicians serve the people. You can change your leader. For me that is so amazing. That's what I want for my country."

Just as the clock strikes five, I come to the politics of Sudan. Jal can now break his fast and he nips off to buy some nuts and a flapjack, which he shares with me. For the rest of the interview we talk between mouthfuls about what is going on back home. He analyses the difficulties of his country: "Sudan's problems have never been with the people but with the politicians". I ask him if he is optimistic about the forthcoming elections. "First of all it is very exciting. But I worry. There could be another war. There are now SPLM soldiers in the North. The South would be wiped from the map and now the North would be affected too. But there's still a good chance for peace". It occurs to me that Jal perfectly personifies that chance. He remembers the horrors of war yet he bears no malice.

This interview was conducted in 2009

About the author:

Peter graduated from the University of Sussex and School of Oriental and African Studies. He has worked as a teacher, communications officer for an NGO in Sudan, freelance writer, researcher and government advisor. Peter plays squash and tennis; he enjoys cookery greatly; and he recently bought a flat in Streatham.